LEAVING HOME

LEAVING HOME

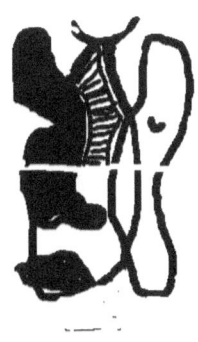

A NOVEL BY

RICHARD LEITER

ISBN: 979-8-9876013-0-3

Front Cover Photo by Levent Simsek: *Man in black jacket sitting on chair*
Back Cover Photo by Laura Paredis: *A wake in the sea*
Book Design: Richard Leiter

for the marooned

1. THE ADORABLE GENIUS

I was seventeen years old at the time. I was in the twelfth grade—a high school senior. I was just a week shy of graduation; and in a mere twelve weeks after that would be leaving home to attend college—one of those terribly terribly expensive monstrosities located on the outskirts of Bean Town—which both my controlling father and my controlling mother were looking forward to with trepidation. On that particular warm, humid Monday morning my controlling mother was unusually "trepidated." She was regarding me with considerable scrutiny—with a kind of Svengali-like concentration—trying her damnedest to seize control of my admittedly wavering adolescent attention span so that the things which she was trying to impress upon me could have at least a *tiny* chance of sinking in.

"And *then*, Franklin," my mother said to me, pointing her long, skinny, baubled index finger up to the stucco ceiling for dramatic effect, "if you don't know who your people are—where they've come from— who they've been with—"

"What do you mean, Ma—'who they've been with'?"

"You know…. Who they've been with. Who their contacts have been."

"Well, what do you mean by the word 'contacts' exactly? You mean like… business contacts? You mean like business associates?"

"No, moron. I mean partners. I mean contacts as in previous sexual partners."

'Sexual partners, huh?"

"Yeah."

"Sexual partners…. Sexual partners…." I appeared to be lost in space for a couple of seconds. Befuddled. Confused. Deliberately obtuse or slow-witted. The term "sexual partners" was like a foreign language to me. Like Greek or Swahili. Or Hindi. Or Mandarin.

"What exactly does that term mean, Ma?"

"What term?"

"You know…. 'Sexual partners.'"

"You know perfectly well what it means, Franklin."

"I'm afraid not."

"Stop being a wise ass."

"Who's being a wise-ass? Am I being a wise ass? I thought I was asking you a legitimate question."

"Alright, that's enough."

"What's enough?"

"I said STOP!"

My mother shouted the word STOP! at me. But I didn't stop. I kept going. I kept going and going… and going… and going—until eventually, I drove her crazy.

"I give up," she said. "You win," she said. "You win and I lose," she said. "Are you happy now?"

"About what?" I said.

"I try talking to you like a mature person," she said. "Like a mature, reasonable, sensible person. And what do you do to me, son?"

"What do I do to you, Ma?"

"You spit in my face. *You spit right in my face!*"

"I'm not spitting in your face, Ma."

"No! You're spitting on me! You're mocking me! You're spitting on me *and* mocking me. Like it's all just some big joke!"

Okay, okay. So maybe I was spitting on her. Just a little bit—just a teensy weensy bit. So big deal. My mother deserved it. If you treat me like a fucking rube, then that's exactly right. I'm going to spit on you. I'm going to spit on you and I'm going to keep spitting on you.

So much for our first "sex talk." Not really much of a sex talk, now was it? A nothing sex talk. An aborted sex talk. An anti-sex talk. A "sex talk interruptus." Not to worry, however. There would be other sex talks. Other exhortations and dire warnings... graphic descriptions—diagrams, even—concerning the omnipresent, insidious dangers of unbridled concupiscence—especially in teenagers. The diseases.... The disgusting diseases.... The unwanted pregnancies.... Oh! The horror!! Actually—come to think of it— there really weren't any other subjects covered during the course of these little stink bombs. It was always either the disgusting diseases or else the unwanted pregnancies—or else *both* things. Usually both things. I mean, why cover just the one thing when you can double your pleasure by covering both of them? Makes sense, right?

Yeah. Right.

My mother—you might say—took kind of a dim view concerning you know what.

***

The next sex talk went better. Not a lot better. But a little better. My mother—a bright woman—quickly learned from the first sex talk not to take my disingenuousness quite so seriously. Not to get flustered by it. Not to get rattled by it. To become immune to my little shenanigans and to remain focused on THE MAIN OBJECTIVES which—once again—basically boiled down to:

1) Strongly discouraging her idiot offspring from ever engaging in sexual intercourse; and

2) If that didn't do the trick, then trying to make *even the concept* of sexual intercourse so goddamned fucking scary so that I would *never*—not even in a million years—ever want to have anything whatsoever to do with it.

During the second sex talk my mother said to me:

"You can wind up with gonorrhea. Do you hear me, Franklin? GONORRHEA!"

"Yeah, I hear you, Ma. Loud and clear. I can wind up with GONORRHEA."

"Gonorrhea is really terrible. Urination becomes extremely painful. You can become sterile, Franklin. *Totally sterile!*"

"No shit, Ma."

"Yes shit. It's one of most revolting diseases known to Man."

"Is it worse than cancer?"

"Well, it can be."

"How about heart disease?"

"Well, it can cause heart disease."

"How about smallpox?"

"No, not smallpox. Smallpox is a different matter. But gonorrhea can also kill you. If left untreated, it can cause *massive* damage."

"Like becoming sterile, huh?"

"That's correct."

"And like getting heart disease, right?"

"Right."

"Gee, Ma. It sounds awful."

"Oh, it is, son. It's *extremely* awful. It's extremely awful and extremely dangerous."

"Well, it certainly sounds like it's extremely dangerous. What's it called again?"

"Gonorrhea."

"How do you spell it?"

My mother spelled it for me.

"G...."

"G...."

"O...."

"O...."

"N...."

"N...."

"O...."

"O...."

"R...."

"R...."

"R again...."

"R again...."

"H...."

"H...."

"E...."

"E...."

"A...."

"A! GONORRHEA. Okay. Got it, Ma!"

It was just like a miniature spelling bee. First you spelled the word and then you said the word. And then you quietly waited for the judge's decision. Oh, I just loved spelling bees! I just couldn't get enough of the suckers. Being tested on your ability to spell multi-syllabic—often obscure—words which you were probably never even going to use at anytime during the course of your life was one of the few things that I was actually good at.

At that point in our second "sex talk" we proceeded to move on to other venereal diseases. Like, say... syphilis, for example. Now there was a good one. No. There was a *great* one! Syphilis was like... The Royal Flush—The Atomic Bomb—of venereal diseases. Man, if you contracted syphilis, then you were really fucked. What a nightmare! All of those tiny little ticking time bombs—spirochetes, I think they called 'em—eating away at your entire spinal column. Moving up the column—wreaking havoc with it. Making chocolate pudding out of your delicate brain matter. What a way to go, huh? Death by chocolate pudding. Death by gelatinized, mushy oatmeal....

So syphilis definitely got The Academy Award for being Best Actor In A Venereal Disease. But there were other actors—not as flashy perhaps—not exactly what you'd call "the stars" of the show—but important players nonetheless. Like... say... Chlamydia, for example. Ah, yes. Chlamydia. Fair Chlamydia. Or Hepatitis B. Or Trichomoniasis. Or herpes simplex. Or human papilloma virus. Or scabies. Or yeast infections. Or genital warts. Or pubic lice....

"Pubic lice, huh? You mean crabs?"

"Yes. That's right, Franklin. I mean crabs...."

At that point my mother described them to me in excruciatingly exquisite detail—the crabs, I mean. The pubic lice. Their tiny little crab-like arms. Their tiny little crab-like legs. Their tiny little crab-like pincers or claws that would dig into your tender flesh like tiny little miniature grappling hooks and then hold on for dear life. Oh, and the eggs they laid! Oh, and the blood they drank! Horrible. Just horrible. And the people who had them—even *more* horrible. Even *more* revolting and even *more* disgusting than the lousy parasites which they blithely hosted. People, Ma said to me. Ignorant people.... Stupid people.... Oh, these stupid people were like foolish children, she said. Like irresponsible, foolish children who did irresponsible, foolish things. And then they suffered for the things they did. Oh, they suffered.... They suffered! They knew pain. They knew sorrow. They knew misery. Regret. Which was precisely why, Ma proceeded to explain to me, it was so terribly terribly terribly important for a young person such as myself, who had a bright, promising future ahead of him, to exercise a little self-restraint in his various "interactions" with "stupid people." Self-restraint was the key ingredient here. Self-restraint.... Self-control.... Having discipline.... Having principles. Having principles—I mean *real* principles—not just fake, phony, "pretend" principles like the ones which politicians were always blathering about when they were trying to win your vote prior to Election Day—these true principles were our only moral compasses in an essentially rudderless, amoral society.

"You're a person with principles, aren't you, Franklin?" Ma said to me then, after she'd finished "The Lecture."

"Oh, sure, Ma. Absolutely. I've got lots of principles. Millions of 'em."

"Well, you don't have to say it *that* way."

"Say it what way?"

"Like you're making a joke out of it."

"Who's making a joke out of it?"

"You are."

"No, I'm not! I'm not making a joke out of anything."

"Well, it certainly sounded like you were making a joke out of it."

"Rest assured, Ma. I was being serious. I was being totally serious and not making a joke out of it."

"*Totally* serious?"

"Yes. *Totally* serious."

"Swear to God, Franklin?"

"Yes. Swear to God, Ma."

Thankfully Ma shut her trap at that point. However, she still continued to eye me skeptically. Was I telling her the truth, she wondered? Was I being sincere? Or was I still up to my old tricks? She wasn't sure.... She wasn't sure.... She was *almost* sure but not *completely* sure. And there was the rub. She wasn't *completely* sure. She was never completely sure about anything I told her. Poor Ma. Poor Ma. Ma really hated ambiguous people. People who, whenever they said things, always seemed to be saying *other* things. With other meanings. With *hidden* meanings. Ma preferred simplicity in people. People who didn't have even an ounce of guile in them. Ma was the only person who was supposed to be entitled to guile. But not other people. Perish the thought! Case in point: I had a friend who lived across the street from us, in an apartment building which looked exactly like ours did. Let's call this friend "Bill." Well, Ma really liked Bill. I mean she really, really, really *liked* the guy. Bill read *The New York Times* and studied the stock market. He and his father, a Vietnam vet turned insurance actuary, had long cozy fireside chats about the inverse correlation between bond prices and interest rates; and the deleterious effects which inflation had upon currency value. I suppose that if Bill's father had been a traveling minstrel instead of an insurance actuary, Bill and his father would have had long cozy fireside chats about the rewarding world of Traveling Minstrelry as opposed to the vicissitudes of High Finance. Similarly, if Bill's father had been, say, an international jewel thief, then I suppose that Bill—being Bill—would have coincidentally gotten an enormous hard-on for the glamorous world of International Jewel Thievery. And, finally, if Bill's father had been a methamphetamine or heroin drug dealer—well, you get the idea. The career paths were literally endless. Poor Ma. Poor Ma. To have given birth to such an ambiguous child.... Bill should have been her child. Simple Bill. Guileless Bill. Practical Bill. Bond Market Bill. It says in The New Testament that the simple and the guileless shall inherit the earth—that is... if you interpret "simple" and "guileless" as being synonymous with "meek"—which I do—which I definitely do—because I, for one, have certainly never encountered any so-called "meek" members of the human species for whom the phrases "extremely simple" and "extremely guileless" couldn't be substituted with perfect accuracy. They were *all* extremely simple and extremely guileless. Every one of them. No exceptions. Only... what about all of those other people? You know what I'm talking about when I say "other," right? I mean all of those "problematic," "pesky" people who just don't seem to fit conveniently into "The Meek Category." I mean the ambiguous ones. I mean the enigmatic ones. I mean the extremely complicated and hard-to-figure-out ones. What will become of them, I wonder? What exactly will *they* inherit? Will they *also*—these "hard-to-figure-out" ones—inherit a nice chunk of whatever's left of the earth after humanity has had its fill of raping it; or will these extremely complicated individuals be unceremoniously *dis*-inherited precisely because of their infernal "peskiness?"

Inquiring minds need to know.

I personally am inclined to believe that such "extremely complicated individuals" will be unceremoniously *dis*-inherited—because I have a very, very strong suspicion that both The Old & New Testaments consider ambiguity and complexity to be nothing more than forms of willfulness. And what is willfulness, after all, if not just another form of disobedience? And what is disobedience, after all, if not the very sum and substance of... SIN?

Now, I could be wrong about this—obviously. I mean, I'm not infallible, like—say—The Pope is. What The Pope says is always infallible because The Pope is... well... you know... THE POPE.

However, what *I* say is always *not* infallible because I—alas—am just ME—your humble word-slinger and fledgling novelist. Nevertheless.... *Nevertheless....* In spite of the fact that I am not The Pope, but merely a word-slinging, fledgling novelist; I still stand by my rather bleak prediction concerning the fate of the extremely complicated and, therefore, "willful" among us. As a matter of fact, not *only* do I still stand by it, but I would even go so far as to say unequivocally and without hesitation that for me *not* still to stand by it would be tantamount to a form of lunacy—I guess you could call it "The Lunacy Of The Wishful Thinker" or "The Lunacy Of The Cockeyed Optimist"—and I, for one, am not an optimist. Nor am I a pessimist. I am a realist. I see the world not as I would *like* to see it, but as it truly is—which, unfortunately, is extremely depressing. You see, the plain, simple, depressing truth of the matter is that extremely complicated individuals just aren't welcome here—on Planet Earth. It's just that simple. They aren't welcome here. They are m o c k e d h e r e. They are reviled here. They are persecuted here. They are The Foe here. Why The Foe, you ask? Why not The Friend? Why not The Ally? Why not The Asset? Who knows? Who the fuck knows? That's just the way it is, unfortunately. That's just the way the game is played here. Maybe—on other planets—extremely complicated individuals are treated differently. More intelligently. With the respect they deserve. With admiration, even. On this planet, however—forget it. It just ain't gonna happen—*ever*. First come the strange looks. Then comes the active hostility. Then comes the frank revulsion. And then—after the frank revulsion—comes... well... you know what comes after the frank revulsion, don't you? Bad stuff comes. Dicey stuff. Drastic measures which will make your toes curl.

This is why it is so terribly important on this very special, unique planet of ours for the extremely complicated to pretend they're simple; and for the extremely ambiguous to pretend they aren't.

Survival first. Glory, later.

***

Ok. Now this. This goes back even further. One of my earliest memories of familial dysfunction. I have been an alien upon The Earth now, trying my damnedest to successfully impersonate one of these botched, savage human beings, for a mere seven complete solar cycles; and I now find myself sitting bemusedly—if not actually downright *sullenly*—on that infernally noisy, uncomfortable, awkward, and just plain ridiculously *neurotic*, anally retentive 1950's-style plastic slip cover of my parents' Bronx apartment fabric sofa. My earthly mother—bless her earthly heart—apparently is in one of her "house-buying moods" again. She wants to buy a new house. A new house in the suburbs. With a nice backyard—maybe half an acre—and an outdoor deck for all of those family barbecues. In addition to the nice backyard—maybe half an acre—and to the outdoor deck for all of those family barbecues, she would also like to have a swimming pool. Ah, yes! The gated swimming pool. Not one of those round, ugly "tubs," mind you, that resemble watering holes for circus elephants—but a *real* swimming pool. You know.... Kidney-shaped. That was one of my mother's favorite pet peeves—one of the biggest crosses that she had to bear: not owning her own home. Being a renter. Being a "loser." Being one of the un-anointed, huddled masses who lived in claustrophobic, pinched apartment buildings like so much depersonalized human chattel. Ugh! What an insult! What a shameful affront to the human spirit! Renter's money, Ma said, was blood money. It was sucker's money. It was fool's money. It was money which—by its very nature—was designed to keep you in perpetual bondage—to keep you running around in endless circles in your little rat wheel or your little rat cage. You owned nothing—you had nothing. You worked—but you had nothing to show for it. Ah, but homeowners—that happy breed—didn't shell out blood money. Homeowners built equity. They had property. Which had *value*. And property values always increased. They never decreased—or only rarely. And even when they did decrease, it was only temporary. It was only transitory. Which was why, when you finally "saw the light" and decided to take that long-overdue swan dive into The Great Olympic Swimming Pool of Home Ownership—like so many disillusioned, fed-up renters before you—you stayed "in the pool." You didn't quit "the pool." You didn't swap "the pool" for another "loser rat cage" whenever times got just a little tough. "Tough" was temporary. "Tough" was transitory. You had to remember that. It was only transitory.

All of the smart people knew this. They all bought things; they all *owned* things.

Owning things—possessing things. That was the way that millionaires became billionaires.

My father, however, didn't want a new house. With houses came headaches—lots of headaches. Aggravation. And my father didn't exactly have what you might call "a hard-on" for aggravation. It was one of his least favorite, fun things—along with plumbing and aluminum siding. These things repelled him—aluminum siding repelled him. Lawn mowers repelled him. Heating oil repelled him. Driveways repelled him. And the word "contractor" gave him apoplexy. "These bunko artists make me sick!" was my father's usual, stock response to even the slightest, casual allusion to contractors and to home improvement. "They're leeches, I tell you. They're nothing more than a bunch of parasites!" Anyone with a set of power tools and a Ford pick up truck was "a goddamned parasite." Ditto for electricians. Double ditto for plumbers. Plumbers were the worst offenders. They were the slimiest of opportunists, preying upon the vulnerabilities of the unsuspecting, fearful homeowner like a cabal of grifters who had found the perfect mark—intimidating you into believing that if—God forbid—you didn't hire them—and hire them quickly, too—on the double!—that your beloved hearth and home was going to blow up; or that it was going to disappear forever into some great, cavernous, infernal sink-hole while you and the missus were soundly sleeping. Bastards. Slimy bastards. Unscrupulous vultures.... Bottomless money pits.... My mother obviously disagreed—disagreed strongly—disagreed *vociferously*—with Dad's categorical,

11

global rejection of the whole "Welcome, Dear Friend, To The Elysium Fields Of Home Ownership" scam. She thought that Dad was just being cheap—a really cheap, sick, paranoid son of a bitch who thought that everybody in the entire universe—including her, of course—was out to ruin him.

"Listen, Freddie," she used to say to my father. "Wake up and smell the coffee, will you? Believe it or not, people buy houses. They actually buy houses and hire contractors and live to tell the tale. Nobody dies from it."

"How do you know that nobody dies from it?"

"Nobody dies from it. Nobody hangs himself. You hire a contractor to fix stuff, and then when he's finished fixing it—you pay the guy. That's it. It isn't brain surgery."

"Yeah, but just how much do you actually pay the guy? Answer me that, Doris. How much do you pay him? Do you pay him hundreds of dollars? Do you pay him thousands of dollars? Do you pay him *tens of thousands of dollars*, Doris?"

"It all depends, Freddie, on what he's fixing."

"Well, I don't have *tens of thousands of dollars*, Doris, to piss away on these goddamned parasites. Let 'em peddle their wares somewhere else. Let 'em bleed some other asshole dry...."

It would go on in that vein. Back and forth. For hours and hours.... What a riot. I mean... I thought that it was riot anyway—seeing the two nut jobs go at it—although I'm pretty sure that they didn't see it that way. They took it seriously. Like it actually meant something.

Cancer—now that's something. Lou Gerhig's Disease—now that's something. Beethoven's Fifth—now that's something. What was this, however? What do you call this? Life is fraught with tragedy—for sure. But it's also trivial. It's also extremely trivial. Recently I had to get my driver's license renewed. Stood on line at the DMV for the better part of a half an hour. There was a fat lady standing in front of me who was arguing with her teenager daughter. About how she had to start paying for her own gas & insurance—OR ELSE! The person in back of me smelled bad. He was wearing a pair of plaid pants and a sweat jacket. The front of the sweat jacket said "HI, STRANGER!" and the back of it said "I WANT TO SEX YOU UP, BABY!" Tragic, right? Really tragic. I'm surprised I didn't run into my parents there....

Anyway.... There we are. The old man and his youngest offspring. Right after the big skirmish, the big tiff about slimy contractors and thousands of dollars being flushed down the toilet. We are walking along The Grand Concourse. A nice day. Very sunny. Lots of people scurrying about. Lots of faces—average faces. Sad faces. Miserable faces. Angry faces. Numb faces—faces, in other words, which seem to betray some sort of vague ennui or disenchantment with life. In this respect, my father and I are no different. We fit right in there, with the rest of humanity. Confused and bewildered. Overwhelmed. Hurt, basically—wounded irreparably—all superficially pasted over with a thin veneer of inept stoicism. But then suddenly—out of nowhere—in a rare moment of vulnerability—perhaps precipitated by that sense of lassitude which would often plague Dad after sparring with Ma—my father allows me a fleeting glimpse into the troubled waters beneath his calm exterior as he says to me rather cryptically but at the same time *not* cryptically:

"There is more to life, son, than owning a house in the suburbs. Houses and procreation are not the end-all and be-all."

"What are the suburbs, Dad?" I ask my father.

"That's where people go to buy houses, son."

"And what's that other thing—procreation?"

"Procreation is—" and my father smiles at this point.

"Procreation is... *aggravation*."

"Aggravation?"

"Yeah. Headaches. You know what headaches are, don't you, Franklin?"

"Yeah. Sure, Dad. That's when your head hurts."

"That's right, son. That's it exactly. Procreation is a huge headache."

Once again my father smiles at me. He looks happy enough. He looks *extremely* happy. But something—I don't know what exactly—intuition, maybe; a kind of "sixth sense," maybe—tells me that he's really *not* happy. That he's really something *other than* happy. Irritable, maybe. Angry, maybe. Disillusioned, maybe. World-weary, maybe. Something like that, anyway. Something... not pleasant.

It doesn't exactly take an Edgar Cayce to understand this about my father. I mean, anybody can understand it. Even a non-psychic. Even an average person. And—like I say—I'm only seven years old. I'm just a seven-year-old average person.

***

My mother—as you've probably guessed by now—was not exactly what you'd call "a well woman." She was a sick woman. She was a disturbed woman—even though she seemed as normal as the next person to most people who knew her slightly. But then... a lot of serial killers are like that, aren't they? They seem the very picture of mental health, of moral rectitude and moral fiber—wouldn't hurt a fly, right?—volunteered at the local animal shelter—had a pet poodle named Mrs. Thatcher—until that unspeakably abominable, revolting day, that is, when you finally read about them in all of the newspapers. You know.... "POSTAL WORKER OF SEVENTEEN YEARS CONFESSES TO CANNIBALIZING TEENAGE CO-EDS" or "HUMAN SKELETAL REMAINS FOUND UNDER ROSE BUSHES OF RETIRED SOCIAL WORKER AND BOYSCOUT TROOP LEADER." People like that, I mean. Sick people. True. My mother wasn't really a "serial killer" in the conventional, colloquial sense of the term—like a Ted Bundy, say, or a David Berkowitz—but she was almost as bad because she was a serial *soul* killer. Yes. That's right. You heard me correctly. She was a serial *soul* killer, as opposed to being a serial *body* killer. In other words, she would leave the body alone—wouldn't touch the body—wouldn't dream of touching it—but, instead, would channel all of her destructive tendencies into the decimation of a person's psyche.

Ergo, the term "soul killer."

I am pretty sure that when my mother was just a young girl, playing with Barbie dolls and sucking on lollipops, that she didn't dream about being a serial soul killer. Most serial soul killers don't dream about being serial soul killers. They dream about being normal, with normal friends and with normal interests. I am pretty sure that when my mother was just a young a girl, playing with Barbie dolls and sucking on lollipops, that she dreamed about being a teacher. Or a nurse. Or a secretary. Or a dental hygienist. But then—you know…. Shit happens. Bad shit. Funky shit. They become serial soul killers instead of teachers. They become David Berkowitz's instead of dental hygienists. Poor Ma. Poor Ma. I mean… all the woman wanted to do, probably, was become a secretary or a dentist hygienist. And what's so bad about that, huh? What's wrong with becoming a secretary or a dental hygienist? Some of the nicest people in the world are secretaries and dental hygienists. But not Ma. Oh no. The gods had other things—*darker* things—in store for the young girl who was to become my mommy. Sometimes—for whatever reason—the gods do that to certain people. They assign to these people a darker purpose so that they may serve the gods in a darker capacity. Never mind what that capacity is. That's for the gods to know. It's not for us to know. If the gods really wanted us to know what kinds of fun & games they had in store for us, then I suppose they'd tell us—being the gods. Only they don't. They don't tell us. They keep it a secret—this BIG SECRET. They know, and we don't know. And that's it.

We don't know.

This then, in the final analysis, is the considerably softer, gentler, kinder light in which I prefer to see the woman who gave birth to me— not as some emotionally labile, neurotic bitch—not as some gratuitously evil, sadistic shrew—no… not as some millstone or leaden anchor forever wrapped around my skinny neck as I attempted to circumnavigate Life's hidden sandbanks and razor-sharp Great Barrier Reefs; but, rather, as a kind of humble servant—as a kind of loyal, devoted, faithful lackey—whose sole purpose in her earthly existence was to obey the capricious orders of her inscrutable overlords. She was their humble servant, I say. She was their obedient agent. This, I have come to the conclusion, is the only way to see serial soul killers. You have to see them in a cosmic light. You have to see them in a broader context. Of course... you don't really *have to* see them in this "cosmic light" or "broader context" if you don't really want to see them that way. That's up to you. That's entirely your decision. But it definitely does help to see them that way. I mean... I've found it to be helpful, anyway. Otherwise it can be very depressing—bearable but depressing. And the shrink bills will be enormous.

***

Now in addition to being a serial soul killer—that is to say, a person who—for whatever reason—has this overwhelming, overpowering need to make chopped liver out of another's psyche; to make Swiss cheese out of another's spirit; to carve up their sensibilities—their nuanced thoughts and their delicate feelings—like a side of prime rib in a Chicago slaughterhouse.... In addition, as I say, to being one of these stone-cold serial soul killers sent down to the Earth by the inscrutable gods in order to fulfill some dark purpose—my mother was *also* (as if that wasn't enough) an incredibly asinine, pretentious snob. Yes. That's right. You heard me correctly. She wasn't *just* a serial soul killer. She was also a snob—and a pretty big one. I guess that would make Ma either "a big snobbish serial soul killer" or else "a big serial soul-killing snob"— depending upon your point of view. If you thought that Ma was primarily a serial soul killer and that her being an incredibly asinine, pretentious snob was just a serendipitous added perk, then I suppose that the former description would be more to your liking; whereas, if you thought that Ma was primarily an incredibly asinine, pretentious snob, and that her being a serial soul killer was the actual perk, then it stands to reason that you would favor the latter description. Either way is fine with me. I personally prefer the former description since I basically see Ma as a serial soul killer. But—hey—that's just me. You go right ahead and choose your own description.

Anyway…. Just to recap…. My mother—the serial soul killer—was also this incredibly asinine, pretentious snob when she wasn't busy being a serial soul killer. I don't know what else you'd call it exactly—this… *thing* of hers… this grotesque mask of hers which, going as far back as I can remember, she wore with immense pride—pugnaciously, even. Oh, she was a snob alright! No question about it. —And not only was she a tremendous snob, she was probably *the biggest* snob that I ever met in my life—far snobbier than your average snob—your everyday, ordinary, run-of-the-mill, normal snob— particularly when it came to the education of her two adorable genius children—Gregory Cohen (the older genius) and Franklin Cohen (the younger genius). My father, mind you, was also a snob—but not nearly as big a snob as my mother, The Queen, was. On a scale of 1 to 10 in terms of snobbishness, I would give my father a 7 or an 8. Or maybe a 9, even—although giving him a 9 would kind of be pushing it. My mother, however, I would give an 11. I would give her a 12. A 15. A 60. A 500. She was that kind of snob. She was like… the Babe Ruth of pretentious snobs.

Just to give you an idea of the kind of tremendous snobbishness that we're talking about here, just let me say this about it: My mother, when we were growing up, would say inappropriate, bizarre things to us, dating back to around the time when my brother Gregory and I were still in grade school. She would say inappropriate, bizarre things to us like:

"When both of my two adorable genius children—that means you, Gregory, and you, Franklin—finally get accepted into that Harvard shit hole, we shouldn't have to pay a penny for it. Do you hear me, boys? NOT A PENNY! If those Harvard jerks can't appreciate the *huge* favor that we're gonna be doing for 'em, then they don't deserve us. *They're not worthy of us!*"

Or:

"Do either of you two nitwits have *even the slightest idea* of what a one-hundred-and-thirty-seven I.Q. means? Do you? I mean... DO YOU? That's Harvard material—that kind of an I.Q. That's Einstein material. *Plastic Surgery material....*"

Or:

"If both of my two adorable genius children—with their unbelievably amazing brain power—don't get full scholarships to go to Harvard, I'm going to go over to Sammy Wertheimer—that chain-smoking *meshugana* gun nut who does Daddy's taxes for him every April—borrow his .45, and blow my brains out all over the carpet with it...."

Talk about feeling pressured. I felt pressured. I felt anxious. I was a nervous wreck all the time. Diarrhea, baby, big time. I mean Big Time. I mean HUGE TIME. My older brother developed an incipient stomach ulcer. Only a year shy of junior high school and already the kid's seeing stomach specialists. Apparently my brother wasn't able to handle that kind of pressure any better than I was able to—and Gregory, mind you, was supposed to be my "rock." My island of sanity in a parental ocean of doo-doo. Well, so much for keeping up appearances, huh? Even the "rocks" among us aren't made out of stone.

Continuing on now with the Harvard fixation....

My mother, the serial soul killer—that is to say, the big snobby serial soul killer; or—for those of you who prefer it the other way—the big serial soul-killing snob—would often, in her incredible snobbery, go to extraordinarily insane lengths in order to ensure that her youngest adorable genius offspring—that is to say, MOI—your humble author—became an absolutely cracker-jack, superlative test-taker. Cracker-jack, superlative test-taking, after all, was an exceedingly important part of scholastic life. It was without a doubt the most significant—the most influential—single factor which They Who Had Been Entrusted With The Task Of Determining One's "Harvard-Worthiness" took into consideration during the course of their deliberations. It was far more important than, say, being able to cure liver cancer—not that being able to cure liver cancer is an insignificant, small thing, mind you. Because it isn't a small thing. It's a big thing. It's an incredibly huge, colossal, gargantuan thing. But let's be honest about the matter, shall we? Let's not kid ourselves. Let's be candid. In The Grand Hierarchy, or The Grand Pecking Order, or The Grand Dung Heap of Cosmic Significance, what was liver cancer, or lung cancer, or even *brain cancer* compared to test taking? Yes…. Test scores were definitely IT. They were The Supreme Court. The final arbiters. The tyrannical judges & juries of quantifiable, measurable value. If you happened to be that type of person—I mean, that type of *wunderkind* or idiot savant who had this freakish knack for acing tests in the same way that Wolfgang Amadeus Mozart had this freakish "knack" for composing masterpieces—then the Ivy Leagues were definitely your oyster. *However…. On the other hand….* If your College Board scores stunk, alas, like a week old dead mackerel, or like a pile of used jockstraps in a high school locker room, then you might as well say *sayonara* to all of your Ivy League School aspirations; and *konnichiwa* to that humbler reality which now awaited you at SUNY Upstate.

Thus has it always been at these hysterically venerated—and therefore absurdly costly—purported Bastions Of Higher Learning. And thus shall it always be, I would hazard to guess; for as long as these hysterically venerated—and therefore absurdly costly—purported Bastions Of Higher Learning continue to be held in such… over-inflated, hysterical regard. Their inflexible traditions and inflexible policies have been chiseled into the same limestone which bears the faded likeness of Ozymandias. And Ozymandias, as we all know, was certainly venerated for many centuries.

My mother—a demented woman—but also an exceedingly intelligent, shrewd, determined one who could have had a satisfying, stellar career in just about… *anything* other than child-rearing—understood this about Harvard and the other schools on her "A" list.

19

She understood all too well the inherently jaded nature of these institutions. Just how fussy they all were. Just how finicky. How inflexible. And so, armed with that empowering knowledge—with that incredibly prescient, *heightened awareness* of the tremendously disproportionate amount of weight given by the arbiters of these institutions to exceptionally superior, outstanding test scores—my mother immediately began taking the appropriate prophylactic countermeasures by snatching up just about every "fake," "practice" test out there—every "sample" test—every "prep" test—every "dry run" test—every "study guide"—for me to sink my teeth into like the Great White from the movie *Jaws.* "Study m'boy. Study. Steel yourself and then prosper. Build those S.A.T. muscles and then waltz into Harvard like Fred Astaire or Gene Kelly. You'll be singin' in the rain, son. Just you wait. It *will* happen...." You are, no doubt, thoroughly familiar with the kinds of "fake," "practice" tests I'm talking about. Every bookstore on the planet has them. Shit. Every bookstore on *other planets* probably has them as well—along with testimonial after testimonial blathering about how freaking great they are. You know.... "My child was a fucking moron before I bought him *Scheisseberger's Official Study Guide.* And now look at him. He's an absolute genius! Lives in Westport. Owns a Ferrari. Runs a highly profitable string of whorehouses with branches in New York, Berlin, Munich, Paris, Amsterdam, Stockholm, London and Barcelona...." or "Before my husband and I bought Timmy your incredible *Ninety-Seven Nifty Secrets To Becoming An S.A.T. Superstar*, he was a compulsive masturbator with Attention Deficit Disorder. *Now, however*, thanks to your *Nifty Secrets*, he is a biochemist working for Mandingo, and is just now putting the finishing touches on a brand new form of bean curd which will increase male sterility by approximately 70%...." You get the idea, right? It was a big, big cottage industry. My mother would spend a considerable amount of her weekly allowance on this expensive snake oil. In fact, she would spend *so* much of her weekly allowance on it so that my father—who hated snake oil almost as much as he did slimy contractors—would often scream at her at the top of his lungs for being such an incredibly gullible and naive jackass. My mother, however, remained undeterred. She remained steadfast in her fanatical belief that the acquisition of these practice materials would lead ultimately to Harvard Territory. And so to that end, we pressed on. Together, the two of us would devote an hour each weeknight and two hours on the weekends to these supposedly brain-building educational study guides so that Franklin Cohen—that adorable genius of hers— could prove for once and for all that he was the equal of Einstein. Mr. Franklin Albert Einstein Cohen. Yeah! With my trusty #2 Ticonderoga pencil in hand, its tip poised in mid-air over a nauseatingly well-intentioned series of extremely unassuming sneaky questions (the kinds of extremely unassuming "sneaky" questions, you understand, which had been expressly devised by the very sneakiest of people in order to get The Adorable—albeit latent—Genius to think better—to think smarter—to think faster—to think *sneakier!*), I completed the fake, practice tests in the allotted time (half an hour); whereupon my monomaniacal, fanatical mother proceeded to pour over them as if they were sacred texts.

There were always many, many wrong answers.

"This one is good," she would say. "This one is also good. This one is *very* good. This one is NOT good. OH, MY GOD, FRANKLIN! NOT AGAIN! HOW MANY GODDAMNED FREAKING TIMES ARE YOU GOING TO KEEP FALLING FOR THESE SNEAKY QUESTIONS OF THEIRS?"

"Sorry, Ma. I guess that one got past me."

"OH, IT GOT PAST YOU, HUH?"

"Uh-huh."

"YOU DIDN'T SEE IT, HUH?"

"Uh-uh."

"WHAT—ARE YOU STUPID OR SOMETHING? WHAT— ARE YOU BRAIN DEAD OR SOMETHING? WHAT—HAVE YOU FALLEN ON YOUR HEAD RECENTLY OR SUSTAINED SOME KIND OF MASSIVE HEAD TRAUMA?"

"No, Ma. I haven't fallen on my head recently or sustained some kind of massive head trauma."

"WELL, WHAT'S THE PROBLEM THEN? WHAT'S THE HOLD UP? WHAT'S PREVENTING YOU FROM SEEING THROUGH THIS?"

"I don't know, Ma."

"You don't know?"

"No. I don't, Ma."

"*Jesus, Franklin!*"

My earthly mother would always get just a tad peevish or just a tad "snippy" whenever I was taken in by those notoriously sneaky, trick questions of theirs.

***

Now... my earthly father—bless *his* earthly heart—had his *own* unique, inimitable way of preparing "The Adorable Genius" for the world of THE TEST. One night after work my father brought home a box of vocabulary cards. It was an ordinary enough looking box of the usual cardboard-constructed variety, rectangular in shape, about 10 inches long by 5 inches wide by 3 inches deep—and with a shine on it, some sort of glossy coating. When you removed the cover from the shiny box and took a gander inside of it, you were immediately confronted by a profusion of little index cards. Hundreds upon hundreds of 'em— possibly even thousands of 'em. Neatly stacked. No. *Perfectly* stacked. Why, it was almost as if God Himself had been responsible for all of that perfect card stacking—so harmoniously were they all organized. One little white index card after another little white index card in a nauseatingly repetitive fashion. Maddeningly symmetrical. Maddeningly undeviating—as only inhuman, sterile perfection can be maddeningly undeviating. Whoever had stacked the cards—God, maybe— obviously had had his shit together. Or her shit together. What a stacker! In fact, seeing the cards so perfectly stacked actually made me want to *un*-stack

22

them. Take them out of the box and throw them all up in the air, making a kind of celebratory, orgiastic chaos out of all of that Apollonian, sterile perfection. I didn't do that, however. I resisted the urge. Squelched the impulse. Instead of throwing them all up in the air, making a kind of celebratory, orgiastic chaos out of all of that Apollonian, sterile perfection; I merely took a couple of them out of the box in order to see what exactly was printed on them. Oh, there was a lot of stuff printed on them! Tons of stuff. "Vocabulary" stuff. The first card I took out of the box had the word IATROGENIC printed on it. That was all. There was nothing else. However, when I flipped the vocabulary card over and proceeded to inspect the words which were printed on that side, I read: IATROGENIC (adjective). *Related to illness precipitated by medical treatment or intervention. Example: The patient's sudden demise was due solely to iatrogenic, rather than systemic, causes.* Hm.... Nice to know, I thought. Very nice. So... this big word—IATROGENIC—was really nothing more than a fancy way of saying that The Medical Establishment had fucked up, huh? Which means that the next time I take a medication which actually causes cancer instead of curing it, I can proudly have inscribed on my tombstone:

Used to be...

photogenic.

Took some pills

which made me...

schizophrenic.

Took some more

which made me...

mutagenic.

Now I'm here

which makes me...

iatrogenic.

Iatrogenic.

Yeah. Right.

Then I looked at the next card. Same story. Some big, fancy, five-dollar word printed in capital letters on the front of the card, with the meaning of the word—again—on the back. Now get this: This particular box of vocabulary cards which my father had brought home with him that evening, and whose contents were so harmoniously—possibly even divinely—stacked, stated unequivocally on its glossy cover as well as on each of its four glossy, rectangular sides that the cards which were contained within the box—fifteen hundred of them to be exact—had been manufactured by a company out in Fresno, California which went by the name of The Blarney Stone Corporation. Furthermore, it should be noted that this particular box of vocabulary cards which my father had brought home with him that evening and whose contents were so harmoniously—possibly even divinely—stacked was classified by The Blarney Stone Corporation as being a "Blarney Stone Level II" product; meaning that the words housed within the box were of a more challenging, robust variety than those housed within the "Blarney Stone Level I" series. In other words, the Blarney Stone Level I series was for ordinary, average people with ordinary, average brains; whereas the Blarney Stone Level *II* series—that is to say, the one which my earthly father had so magnanimously procured for me from an extremely well-respected Manhattan bookstore—was for extraordinary, adorable geniuses with extraordinary, adorable brains.

Like I say, my father was also a snob.

At that point my father said to me:

"So what do you think of the box, Frank?"

"What do you mean, Dad?"

"Well, I see you looking at it."

"I don't know, Dad. It's a nice box. I guess."

"Well, you know it's not *just* a box, son."

"Yeah. I noticed, Dad. It looks expensive."

"Well, that's because it is expensive."

"Well, how much did you have to pay for it?"

"Twenty one fifty five."

"Gee, Dad. That's a lot of money."

"Yeah, but it was worth it, son. It was definitely worth it."

"What do you mean, Dad—it was definitely worth it?"

"I mean that this box here is your future, Franklin—and we certainly don't want to skimp on that, do we?"

"No, Dad. We certainly don't. Only… what exactly does that mean?"

"What?"

"What you just said now—about my future."

"What?"

"I mean, how does this box here have anything to do with it?"

"Oh, it's got a lot to do with it."

"How so, Dad?"

"Well, just think about it for a second, Franklin."

"Okay, Dad. I'm thinking about it."

"*Well*, Frank?"

"Well what, Dad?"

"Don't you see it, son?"

"I'm afraid not."

My father groaned then; he groaned loudly. My father would often groan and frequently roll his eyes whenever ding bat failed to grasp something.

"Okay. Let me spell it out for you, Genius," my father said to me then in a most unconvivial manner. "Let's say that you're applying to Harvard, Genius."

"Okay. So I'm applying to Harvard."

"And let's *also* say—just for argument's sake—that there are like…. twenty five thousand *other* guys who are also applying for admission to Harvard."

"Okay. So there are all of these *other* guys. So now what? I still don't get it."

"Well, don't you think, Frank, that if you're *the only guy*—out of twenty-five thousand *other* guys—who knows what an obscure word like 'iatrogenic' means, that that's going to make you really stand out

25

from the rest of the crowd?"

"Yeah, I suppose so."

"You *suppose* so?"

"Well.... I mean if the people at Harvard specifically *ask me* if I happen to know what the word 'iatrogenic' means, well then—yeah—I suppose I'm probably going to knock their socks off. But why on earth would they ever ask me that? I mean... it's not like applying to Harvard is the same thing as being a contestant on *Jeopardy!*."

"Ah, but that's where you're wrong, son. That's where you're dead wrong! You see, it's *exactly* like being a contestant on *Jeopardy!*. Don't cha get it, Frank?"

"I'm afraid not."

"Look: Words are like weapons, son. They are like EXTREMELY DANGEROUS, DEADLY WEAPONS! They may not *look* like they're extremely dangerous weapons but—believe me, Franklin—that's exactly what they are."

"So... these words here—in the box...."

"Yeah?"

"They're like knives, huh?"

"Yeah. Kind a."

"They're like spears?"

"Yeah."

"Bows and arrows?"

"Yeah."

"9 mm. Uzi machine guns and Sherman tanks with rocket launchers?"

"Yeah."

"Okay, Dad. Got it!"

My father seemed a little pissed now, even though I had grasped it beautifully.

"I want you to study the words in the box, Frank," he said.

"What?"

"I said I want you to study the words in the box, Franklin."

"But *why*, Dad?"

"I already told you why."

"But this isn't some damned game show."

"Yes, it is."

"No, it isn't!"

"Well, that's your opinion, buddy boy. But I'm still the boss here."

"Dictator is more like it," I mumbled.

"What was that, Frank?"

"Nothing, Dad."

Then, once again, my father said to me:

"I want you to study the words in the box, Frank. Do you hear me, son?"

"Aye aye, Captain!"

My father frowned at me then—not amused. Then he waited. He just… waited.

We both stood there, not saying anything. I guess that pretty much put a cork in the whole "Aye aye, Captain!" Navy shtick.

Well…. At least *I* thought it was funny, anyway.

Then he said to me, after another couple of seconds:

"*I want you to study the words in the box, Frank. You got it?*"

"Yeah. Sure, Dad."

"I want you to study the words in the box *carefully*, son."

"Yeah. Sure, Dad. I'll study them *carefully*."

Finally he said to me:

"I want you to study the words in the box carefully and then I want you to MEMORIZE the words in the box carefully."

"How carefully?"

"*Very* carefully—using exactly the same amount of meticulous care which you would use to commit to memory a combination."

"A combination?"

"Yes. A combination."

"Well, what kind of a combination exactly?"

"You know…. To a bank vault."

"*To a bank vault?*"

"Yeah. A bank vault. You know.... One of those top secret government bank vaults—like Fort Knox, for instance—where all the gold is stored."

"*That* carefully, huh?"

"YES!"

My father gazed at me then—ominously—like he was going to kick my teeth in or punch my lights out if I didn't take "The Fort Knox Analogy" seriously. I pretended, therefore, to take it seriously. I didn't snicker—although I really wanted to. The last time I snickered at Dad, he used his belt on me. It wasn't pleasant.

Then, after the very ominous—the very belligerent—gaze finally dissipated, my father said to me—still ominously:

"I want you to memorize fifty words every day, Frank."

"Check."

"I want you to memorize *sixty* words every day, Frank."

"Check."

"I want you to memorize between *ninety-five* and *a hundred-and-twenty-five* new words every day, Franklin. A hundred-and-twenty-five would be ideal of course, but anything over ninety-five I would consider to be perfectly acceptable."

"That's insane, Dad. Nobody can do that."

"Well, your brother could."

"Yeah, but Greg's sick now. He's got a stomach ulcer the size of Cleveland. You want your other son getting one too?"

"No, of course not. Don't be ridiculous."

"Well, let's be reasonable then and keep it at sixty, shall we? I mean... I'm pretty sure I can do sixty without giving myself a bleeding ulcer."

"Eighty would be better, Franklin."

"No—sixty. I said sixty."

"How about seventy?"

"No—sixty."

"Sixty-five then?"

"*Noooooooo*—SIXTY!"

"Alright, sixty then. Fair enough. Let's shake on it."

We shook on it.

Then he smiled at me.

I smiled back at him.

Then we retreated again to our respective corners.

And so those were the peculiar circumstances under which the proverbial ball started to get rolling—the way that I began to build up and to augment my singularly unimpressive verbal palette; until it finally became— with much prodding and poking and trepidation and anxiety—the highly comical monstrosity which it has since metastasized itself into. Each day I would carefully study my allotted sixty new "Level II" words, memorizing them as I went along; and each day my ability to incorporate them into my ever-expanding, burgeoning vocabulary grew significantly—dare I say *alarmingly*. My repertoire became truly amazing; it became truly phenomenal—freakish, even. I became something of a "word magnet." An adolescent "word magnet." Strange, arcane words would unerringly gravitate towards "The Word Magnet" like celestial bodies of lesser mass gravitating towards celestial bodies of greater mass. And once I had finally succeeded in memorizing my daily quota of Blarney Stone "Level II" words, my daily quota of Blarney Stone "Level II" words would subsequently get "warehoused" in that dank, cobwebbed part of my brain where I was accustomed to warehousing all of my "junk" data—such as, for instance... the little known but terribly important fact that the average weight of a cumulus cloud is approximately 1.1 million pounds; or that the boiling point of water at the top of Mount Everest is 162 degrees Fahrenheit, which is about 50 degrees below its boiling point at sea level; or (my personal, indispensable favorite) that the word "typewriter" is the longest word in the English language which can be spelled using only the top row of an actual typewriter—that kind of "junk" data. Anyway—for what it's worth—I studied those precious words of mine extremely carefully—

extremely *meticulously*—as if my very life depended upon it. "*Periphrastic*," I would, for instance, say to myself over and over and over again until I had finally succeeded in "breaking in" this exceedingly elegant new verbal accoutrement in pretty much the same way that any average red-blooded American teenager might break in a new catcher's mitt. "*Periphrastic.... Periphrastic.... Pertaining to circumlocution or one who is too wordy.*" "*Urticate*," I would then say to myself over and over and over again until it, too, was sufficiently "well-worn." "*To sting, as with nettles; to irritate; to annoy.*" "*Coruscating*," I would finally say to myself with a decidedly self-congratulatory, superior air—knowing full well what an exceedingly small portion of the world's English-speaking population would ever encounter such an exquisite adjective—let alone ever have cause to use it. "*Glistening, gleaming, sparkling or radiating; exhibiting great brilliance of style or technique.*"

Such, then, were the types of "test" words which I studied diligently; industriously; conscientiously; *meticulously*; in strict accordance with the stringent wishes of my well-intentioned but demented father.

My demented mother had her dummy practice tests, and my demented father had his dummy index cards.

Together, we were the lopsided equivalent of a superbly trained tactical fighting unit.

We were like some kind of sick, twisted, neurotic S.W.A.T. team or "Four Stooges" type of Special Forces.

Ma was Moe, of course. And Dad was Larry. And I was Shep. And my brother Gregory—the proverbial jewel of the family—the fair-haired, sensitive, cerebral one.

2. IN THE DOLDRUMS

In the fall of 1971 I enrolled at Tufts University in Medford, Massachusetts. I did not—repeat, *not*—exactly "knock their socks off" at freaking Harvard. Nor did I exactly "knock their socks off" at freaking Yale. Ditto for freaking Princeton. Double ditto for freaking Amherst.

Poor Ma.

Oh, poor Ma.

Oh, poor broken-hearted, demented Ma.

"Hey, Ma," I remember saying to my mother after I had gotten that first disappointing rejection letter from the freaking Mount Everest of all colleges. "Shouldn't you be going over to Mr. Wertheimer about now?"

"What for? What are you talking about?"

"You know. To borrow that .45 of his and blow your brains out all over the carpet with it."

"Shut up. Just... *shut up!* Why don't you go back to your room, moron, and write something in that stupid diary of yours."

"It's not a diary, Ma. It's a journal."

"Oh, excuse me. I mean in your 'journal.' Why don't you go back to your room, moron, and write something in that stupid 'journal' of yours."

"Well, what exactly do you want me to write about?"

"Oh, shut up! Just... SHUT UP!"

"Okay, Ma. No problem. I can see you're upset so I'll just go back to my room now. Bye, Ma. Feel better."

I went back to my room then.

I took out my journal.

I turned to a blank page.

I started to write stuff.

***

I remained at Tufts for four years—for four "pseudo-gregarious" but actually extremely solitary, reclusive years—at the end of which time I re-united with The Two Demented Ones. The Two Demented Ones hadn't changed much during my Roman holiday up in Boston. As a matter of fact, they were exactly the same—no more demented and no less demented; no more snobbish and no less snobbish; no more serial soul killers and no less serial soul killers. They were basically the same, familiar serial soul killers— and that was something at least: that they remained true to their natures.

Upon my homecoming, my mother said to my father:

"Hey, look, Freddie! The big English major!"

My father looked at me and then he said to my mother:

"Well, there's sixty two thousand dollars that I'll never see again thanks to Shakespeare."

My mother corrected my father: "No, Freddie. Sixty *four* thousand."

"No, Doris. Sixty *two* thousand."

My mother and my father began arguing at that point about the exact figure which they had pissed away on the big English major's education.

I opened the refrigerator door and took out a bottle of Pepsi Cola.

I started drinking from the bottle of Pepsi Cola.

I started sipping from the bottle slowly—taking small sips—as if it were fine wine.

Boy, did that bottle of Pepsi Cola ever taste freaking good.

***

After I returned home from Camp Tufts I did nothing. I mean literally *nothing*. I just sat in my old room for hours on end, thinking odd, rebellious, fleeting thoughts. At night I would have recurring dreams. I didn't actually have nightmares, mind you, but these recurring dreams of mine were definitely unsettling. They were like... partial nightmares or semi-nightmares. Many of them seemed to revolve around my not having actually graduated from college—either lacking the required number of credits to do so, or else failing one or more required courses. In still other recurring, unsettling dreams, I would be late for some test—or I would be unable to locate the test room or the test building. Whatever the recurring dream happened to be, however, its common denominator was always FAILURE. I either screwed up in some very obvious way—the way that most losers tend to screw up—or else I was just on the verge of doing so. My dreams were simple. They were guileless. They were ordinary. They were transparent. It didn't take some hundred-and-fifty-dollar-an-hour Park Avenue headshrinker to get the root of their subliminal meaning.

One day—in real life—my mother barged into my old bedroom while I was sitting in it, on the edge of my bed. She seemed agitated—as usual. My mother was always agitated about something. On this particular occasion, however, my mother seemed to be unusually agitated owing to what she considered to be her son's abject, abysmal failure to have procured any sort of gainful employment since returning home from his Alma Mater. In addition, my mother seemed to be unusually agitated owing to what she considered to be the abysmal *absence* of any agitation which was being exhibited on the part of *moi*. The Big English Major seemed calm. The Big English Major seemed cool. The Big English Major seemed collected—very collected—*extremely* collected. Insouciant, even. Insouciance drove Ma nuts. It was the same with insouciance as it was with irony. They were just two sides of the same coin—that is to say, the same perfectly value-less, expendable coin which only English majors seemed to use as currency. English majors.... Philosophy majors.... Drama majors.... You know.... Arty fartsy types. Agitation was where it was at for Ma. It was The Life Force. It fomented movement. The purpose of life was to foment movement. But Death was the absence of movement. Death was insouciance.

"Why the hell haven't you found a job yet?" (That would be Ma of course, being agitated).

"Gee, I don't know, Ma. It beats me."

"It beats you? *It beats you?*"

"Well, people say that we're in a recession, so I guess the recession must be the culprit."

"The recession is not the culprit."

"If you say so."

"I say so."

[Pregnant pause at this juncture, during which mother & offspring stare lovingly at one another, with mutual respect and admiration. Then Ma again—still agitated:]

"Well, you can't just lock yourself up in your room all day long, Frank—I mean with the blinds closed and with the curtains drawn."

"Well, why can't I?" I said.

"Because you just can't. It's not normal."

"Well, what's 'normal,' Ma?"

"Not this. This is deranged, Frank. It's *psychotic!*"

"Psychotic," I should interject at this point, was one of my mother's all-time favorite words—if not her favorite word in the entire universe.

"You see that man over there—the one with the shopping cart?" my mother, for example, would invariably say to me whenever we would be walking together—usually around midtown Manhattan—and a homeless person happened to be drifting past us. "You see that derelict over there? That hobo? That *bum?*"

"Yeah, Ma. I see the bum."

"Well, that bum is PSYCHOTIC. He ought to be locked up in Bellevue."

Or else she would say to me:

"Take that tie off. Immediately! That tie is hideous. It's PSYCHOTIC!"

Or else—oh, yeah—here's a good one:

"Do you really mean to tell me, dear, that you actually *like* this Francis Bacon shit? These raw sides of beef of his? These bashed in, distorted faces of his? These screaming popes and hideous monsters of his?"

"Yeah, Ma. I really like him."

"Well then, you're just as crazy as he is."

"Yeah. Right, Ma. I wish."

"Now Van Gogh was a painter. Renoir was a painter. Monet was a painter. Cézanne was a painter."

"Well—clearly, Ma—Bacon isn't for everyone."

"He's psychotic, I tell you."

"If you say so."

"*Psychotic!*"

That pretty much put a cork on any further discussion about Francis Bacon.

Anyway.... At that point in the conversation—that is to say, after Mrs. Charm had finished implying that A) the real reason why I couldn't find a job wasn't because there were no jobs to be had; but, rather, because I was just too lazy to find one; and that B) in addition to my being just too lazy to find one, I was also mentally incompetent or not quite right in the head—I mean, that's what the word "psychotic" means, doesn't it?—that you're either mentally incompetent or not quite right in the head....

Anyway.... *Anyway....* After Ma had finished slinging just enough obligatory mud in my face in order for her to maintain the pathetic illusion that she was just being my concerned mother rather than some off-the-wall despotic control freak; she finally "got down to brass tacks," as it were, by saying to me in her usual "illusory" voice:

"This has to stop, Franklin."

I said to her: "What has to stop, Mother?"

She said to me: "*This*, Franklin."

"*What*, Mother?"

"You know what."

"No—WHAT?"

—At which point I proceeded to listen to my mother's rather periphrastic explanation as to what exactly constituted the word THIS — or, rather, *one half* of me listened to it; whereas the *other* half—the detached half—the remote half—the insouciant half which didn't originate from this barbaric planet, but which had actually come here from *another* planet; from another world, in another galaxy—studied her laugh lines, and her crows' feet, and her baggy eyes, and her sagging jowls, and all of those other endearing peculiarities which made Ma, Ma and not Venus de Milo.

Oh, how pitiable were these human beings! I secretly thought to myself as I studied her physiognomy. How miserably constructed! How *crudely* constructed—both spiritually as well as physically speaking. Physically speaking, they were like... a joke. They were built to last for—what? Seventy years? Seventy-two years? Seventy-five years? Eighty—maybe? That is to say, eighty—maybe—provided you had one hell of a terrific supplemental insurance plan. And during the course of which—say—eighty years, they were constantly breaking down. Constantly deteriorating. Constantly needing to have their diapers changed, their ostomies changed, their catheters changed, their medications tweaked. And spiritually speaking.... Oh, well.... *Spiritually* speaking.... What a disaster! An even bigger joke! I mean... how could any of these so-called "advanced" Earth creatures ever hope to become truly "spiritual"—and when I write the words "truly spiritual," what I really mean to write is "truly exceptional"—when absolutely everything about their tepid lives positively screamed *UN*-EXCEPTIONAL? Their thoughts positively screamed *UN*-EXCEPTIONAL! Their feelings positively screamed *UN*-EXCEPTIONAL! Their aspirations positively screamed *UN*-EXCEPTIONAL! Hell, even their misery positively screamed *UN*-EXCEPTIONAL!—COMPLETELY ORDINARY!— because if—God forbid—they began to feel even in the least little bit "miserable" for more than like... twenty seconds, then they immediately ran to their nearest mental health professional, who was always more than happy to write them a script for the latest "flavor of the month" antidepressant. Ditto if they began to feel "angry." Ditto if they began to feel "anxious." Double ditto if they became too "rambunctious." You had to take a pill for it; you had to suppress the offending feeling. Feelings, you see—*intense* feelings—were regarded by these sagacious experts in the fields of Human Psychology and Mental Development as rabid animals which needed to be exterminated. In a similar vein, these so-called "advanced" Earth creatures were constantly being inundated by a kind of castrated or neutered music—commonly referred to as "pop" music—which had the same numbing effect as did their pharmaceuticals. And the same went for the Hollywood films they watched. And the same went for the printed matter they read. And most damaging of all was their God—TELEVISION—the ultimate mind-pacifier and spirit-killer. So it doesn't really seem to me—at least from what I've been able to glean, anyway, since my arrival on this becalmed planet—that becoming a "truly spiritual, evolved person" is a viable option for most human beings as long as there are so many governmentally-sanctioned, mass-media promoted, and societally-tolerated drugs around. I mean... you can certainly *say* to yourself that you're a "spiritual" person—and maybe you really are a "spiritual" person—but I just don't see how it's even remotely possible when your entire life is spent ingesting one stultifying, pernicious drug or another.

....Meanwhile, the first half of me—that is to say, the human being half of me; that is to say, *the imposter* half of me—could now hear my mother droning on. Elaborating. Amplifying. Developing or embellishing upon the recurring theme of her composition.

"Your Father and I, Franklin dear, have been talking things over."

"Oh, you have, have you?" I said to Ma.

"Yes, that's right, Franklin," Ma replied.

"Well, what exactly have you been talking about?"

"Why... *you* of course, sweetheart. I mean, what else would we be talking about?"

"Oh, I don't know, Ma. Quantum Physics, maybe.... Central Banking, maybe.... The Hubble telescope.... Vermeer's palette.... You know.... Stuff like that. Simple stuff."

My mother waited until I was quite finished. Then she said to me—and very proudly, too—as if she were one of the physicists working on The Manhattan Project and had just discovered a new way of extracting radio-isotopes from uranium ore:

"Your father and I have come to the conclusion, Franklin, that what you're lacking in life is stimulation."

"Stimulation?" I said.

"Yes. Stimulation."

"Well... what *kind* of 'stimulation'?"

"Intellectual stimulation. *Scientific* stimulation. Stimulation, you know, Franklin, doesn't have to end just because you've earned your diploma."

"Yes. I'm aware of that fact, Ma."

"Well, you certainly don't act like you're aware of it."

"Oh, but I am, Ma."

"Are you? *Really?*"

"Yes, Mother. I *really* am. Now let's dispense with all of the coyness, shall we, and with all of the introductory mumbo-jumbo, and get on with the real reason for this unexpected—albeit delightful—intrusion. Out with it, Ma. Spill the beans. Stop being so periphrastic."

"Periphrastic?"

"It means wordy."

"Who's trying to be wordy?"

"You are. *I'm waiting....*"

I made a very big show then of glancing impatiently at my Spidell wrist watch. Time was ticking away and I was busy. I had things to do. Places to go. People to meet. Mountains to move. My entire schedule was booked solid for the next two and a half to three decades; and my patience—which was extremely limited—was now dangerously close to being depleted: That was pretty much the gist of the message which I was trying to convey to Ma with that impatient glance of mine.

My mother thankfully got the message, being completely out of her fucking gourd of course—emotionally speaking—psychologically speaking—but she still wasn't a fucking idiot. She was a shrewd woman. With a substantial intelligence. —And being a shrewd woman with a substantial intelligence, she immediately dispensed with all of the "mumbo-jumbo" and started speaking to me very plainly, which must have been terribly hard for her—like having to look at a painting by Francis Bacon for more than two seconds without flapping her gums. Oh, the sacrifices that we have to make at times! Oh, the terrible sacrifices! The tremendous discipline....

And so she said to me then—very plainly:

"New York University has a really *excellent* Pre-Med program for non-matriculating college graduates. Did you know that?"

"Uh-uh."

"It starts right after the New Year. January 3rd, I think. Or January 4th. We both think—your father and I—that you would really enjoy this type of program. In fact, we *know* that you would really enjoy it. They have so many *stimulating, exciting* courses and so many *stimulating, exciting* teachers."

"Oh, really?" I said to Ma.

"Yes. That's right, Frank. We've been doing research."

"And I suppose that you and Dad would like me to take a couple of these very 'stimulating, exciting' courses, right?"

"That's right, Frank. We would. We would absolutely *love it* if you took a couple of them."

"Which ones, Ma?"

"Not many."

"Which ones, Ma?" I repeated the question.

"General Chemistry... Organic Chemistry... General Physics... General Biology... Pre-Calculus... Calculus... Statistics... Biochemistry...."

"Holy shit, Ma! That's a lot of courses! And those are some pretty goddamn heavy hitters!"

"Well, not really, dear. It's just the bare minimum."

"The bare minimum?"

"That's right. You would need to take at least 'The Big Eight' before taking the MCAT's and applying to Medical School."

"Medical School? Who said anything about Medical School?"

"Well, that would be the ultimate goal, wouldn't it? Applying to Medical School? I mean to a *good* Medical School? I mean... why else bother taking them?"

"You know, Ma...." I said to my mother then.

"What, Franklin?" my mother said to me.

"I never really liked Science that much."

"What do you mean, Frank, you never *liked* it?"

"I mean I never liked it. It never interested me."

"But it's *very* interesting. It's *extremely* interesting. How can you say that? Your brother *loved* Science."

"Well, that was Greg, Ma. *He* loved it. But I don't. I hate Science."

"You *hate* Science?"

"That's right. I *hate* it."

"But you can't really mean that?"

"No, Ma. I really do."

My mother gazed at me at that point with a rather curious, indescribable admixture of bewilderment, consternation, disbelief, and even amusement—although the amusement component was certainly the least of it. The skin of her weak, decidedly limp, flaccid face seemed to wince in pain simultaneously—coincident with my frank disclosure—as if she were being given an injection of Novocaine just prior to having a cavity filled. That was Ma alright. That was Ma to a tee. Whenever Ma, The Serial Soul Killer, encountered any sort of annoying obstacle—any sort of inconvenient, pesky impediment to her serial-soul-killing machinations—the skin of her face would invariably tighten and wince. The sagging jowls would suddenly become *un*-sagged; the baggy eyes, suddenly *un*-bagged. Why, it was almost as if she would suddenly undergo a sort of "mini-facelift" transformation. She would actually look *young* again. Like her old self. You know.... *Vibrant.*

"So that's *it* then?" Ma said to me.

"Yep. That's it, Ma," I said to Ma.

"So you're just to going to *lie* there, in other words?"

"Yeah, I guess so."

"Doing nothing?"

"Well, that's not really fair, Ma. I mean, I don't exactly do *nothing*. I read books. I take walks. I go to New York on job interviews. This Thursday, for example, I have an interview with Doubleday."

"Ha!" my mother bellowed.

"That's not fair, Ma, and you know it."

"HA!" Ma bellowed again, even louder and more contemptuously. "The day that pigs fly will be the day that some big, fancy New York City publishing house considers hiring your ass. These interviews are a waste of time. They're completely ridiculous. They're psychotic."

"Don't you mean that they're 'futile,' Ma?"

"What's futile?"

"My Publishing House interviews."

"I just said that."

"No you didn't."

"Well, what did I say then?"

"You said 'psychotic'."

"Psychotic.... Futile.... Self-destructive.... What the difference?"

"Oh, there's a difference alright. There's a big difference. Words matter."

"Words are just words, Frank. They don't pay the bills, bubby. Money pays them."

"Well, now that you mention it, Ma...."

"What?"

"The Money Factor...."

"Well, what about 'The Money Factor'?"

"You do realize, of course—don't you, Ma?—that I just graduated

41

from an expensive college."

"No kidding, Frank. I didn't know that."

"No, really, Ma. Just hear me out now."

"YES?"

"I just graduated from what is probably one of most expensive colleges on The Eastern Seaboard. I mean... you and Dad just pissed away a ridiculous sixty-two thousand dollars—"

"—Sixty-*four* thousand dollars, Shakespeare."

"—Okay. A ridiculous sixty-*four* thousand dollars on some totally meaningless college diploma. So do you and Dad really want to spend *another* sixty-four thousand dollars on some hair-brained, crazy scheme to get me to become the next Dr. Kildare?"

"Well, it really wouldn't be as costly as all *that*, Frank. It's just eight, you know."

"Eight what, Ma?"

"Science courses."

"Eight courses.... Six courses.... Two courses.... What the hell is the difference, Ma? I hate Science, okay? I *loathe* Science. I have absolutely no interest whatsoever in numbers or equations or formulas or any of that shit. How many times do I have to tell you?"

"But how can you really *say* that? I mean... how do you *really* know that?"

"Well—like I say, Ma—I just know it. I just *feel* it. I mean... it's not like I'm *trying* to hate Science. I just do. I can't help it."

Once again, the subtle wince. The highly concentrated—albeit fleeting—pain invariably arising out of the confrontation with some maddeningly intransigent, immovable obstacle. I hated Science—Ma loved Science. I contemplated—Ma agitated. There wasn't a hell of a lot that we had in common. We had absolutely nothing in common—notwithstanding genetics.

But my mother wasn't quite finished yet. Being an exceedingly bloodthirsty, tenacious Dracula, she still had miles to go and gallons to suck out of my already blood-depleted, anemic body. Indeed, I am looking up the word "Dracula" in my trusty little pocket dictionary, even as I write it down now; and my trusty little pocket dictionary—which I carry around with me practically everywhere—defines the word "Dracula" thusly: DRACULA: *The eponymous Transylvanian count and vampire in a gothic horror novel by Bram Stoker; a nocturnal ghoul who bites his victims on the neck, drinks their blood, and robs them of their spiritual vitality. Example: Frank's spiritually destitute, emotionally starving, physically deteriorating, and intransigent mother—being the perfect embodiment of an insatiable Dracula—simply refused to accept the fact that Frank hated Science; and therefore tried to convince Frank that he actually LOVED Science*—which was basically what my mother said to me after I'd told her how I really felt about it. She said to me:

"Well, that may not be entirely true, dear. I mean, you might *think* that you hate Science, but do you *really* hate it?"

"Yes, Ma. I really hate it."

"Well... now you're just being difficult."

"No I'm not."

"Yes you are. Because if you *think* that you hate Science, well, then... yes... naturally you're going to say that."

"Say what?"

"That you hate Science—because you've already rejected the idea that you might actually love Science out of hand."

"Ah...."

"But if you *don't* think that you hate Science—if your mind is open to at least *the possibility*—however small!—that you might actually love it...."

"Yes, Ma? Go on."

"Well... you fill in the blanks, dear."

I filled them in then, as Ma had instructed. And it didn't take me very long to do it either. I mean... I was an extremely bright, energetic lad, fresh out of The Ivory Tower; having graduated from my beloved Tufts with the very highest of academic honors. If that didn't qualify me to "fill in the blanks" in record-breaking, lightening speed, then I didn't know what did.

And remember, too, I was an adorable genius.

"Well…. Maybe, Ma," I said to my mother then.

"Maybe what, Frank?"

"*Maybe* I'd love it."

"There! You see, Frank! You finally admit it! Good for you, sweetheart!"

"No I don't, Ma! I admit nothing! All I'm saying is that *theoretically* it's entirely possible that I might love Science—just like *theoretically* it's entirely possible that the sun won't rise tomorrow morning; or that *theoretically* it's entirely possible that JFK was killed by a lone gunman."

"Well, he was killed by a lone gunman."

"Yeah. Sure he was. And I'm Santa Claus."

My mother frowned then. She didn't like that—that little quip of mine about JFK. Then she said to me—still frowning:

"Let me ask you a little question, Franklin."

"Go ahead, Ma. Ask away."

"Did anybody ever tell you, Frank, that you're an extremely pessimistic, depressing person?"

"No, Ma. Only you."

"Well, it's true, Frank."

"No it's not true."

"You know, you acted exactly the same way just before we sent you away to Camp TaHoNee."

"Camp what, Ma? Titicaca?"

"No, Franklin. Camp TA-HO-NEE."

"Oh, yeah. Right. That place."

"You just sulked in your room for three weeks on end—three weeks of endless *kvetching*. You felt nauseous. You threw up. You had chest pains. You had headaches. God! What a hypochondriac. But *then*, when you finally got there, you fell in love with the place. You actually *adored* the place. Well, it can be the same way with this, Frank. You just have eliminate the negative and accentuate the positive. That's all. It's very simple."

"Say, isn't that a line from a Perry Como song, Ma?"

My mother, with her usual & customary magnanimity and largesse, deliberately ignored this last quip of mine; graciously opting instead to take The High Road.

"Opportunities," she merely added. "Opportunities, Franklin.... New experiences...."

"What do mean, Ma—opportunities?"

"I mean when Opportunity knocks, Franklin—"

"Okay, okay. I get it now."

"—let him in, son. Don't ignore him. Open the door and say: Pleased to meet cha!"

"Alright, Ma. You've made your point," I said.

"Do you mean it, Frank? Have I *really* made it—or are you just saying that to get rid of me?"

"I'm just saying it to get rid of you. Whatever it takes, Ma...."

"*How dare you!*"

I thought she'd leave at that point. I really did. I mean... I'd certainly insulted her enough, hadn't I? Been my usual impossible, rude self? But no. Noooooooooooo! No such freaking luck. She just kept going and going and going... and going. No dignity. No shame. No sense of honor. No nothing.

I suddenly realized at that point that I had to go to the bathroom. Very badly.

***

Eventually Ma left. I mean, she *finally* left. Hallelujah. The Bastion Of Certitude was once again The Bastion Of Certitude; and I (that is to say, Super-English-Major-Man) now contemplated my incredible Super-English-Major-Man super powers. I contemplated: My super cleverness. My super sarcasm. My super irony. My super insouciance. Oh, I was a Super-English-Major-Man alright! There was absolutely no fucking doubt about it—for only a Super-English-Major-Man could have been capable of pissing away four years at an expensive college—and not only at an "expensive" college—but at one of the most preeminent ones on The Eastern Seaboard—without having profited from the experience in any quantifiable or measurable way.

I had been an avid reader before college. I had been an avid reader during college. And I was *still* an avid reader—a voracious reader—even after I was done with Tufts.

A cup of coffee still cost me four bits—same as it cost everybody else. And a subway token still cost me the same, too. I mean... they didn't have *two* separate kinds of token prices in New York: One for the English Majors and one for the *non*-English Majors; one for the avid readers and one for the *non*-avid readers. It's shocking—I know. It's mind-boggling—*I know!* Ah, the injustice of it. Ah, the ignominy of it. Ah, the insanity of it.

Insanity, thy name is Rapid Transit.

***

Over the next several disgusting weeks, Ma really turned up the heat big time on the whole N.Y.U.-Pre-Med-Course thing. Her constant pestering—her agitation—which had always been a thing of beauty, was now catapulted to even greater heights—to even more exalted, remote regions—where the thin air was even thinner; and the blue skies, bluer still. My father, on the other hand, didn't really have much to say about it—but then... Dad didn't really have much to say about anything unless you coaxed him first. You had to "encourage" Dad to come out of himself. You had to say to Dad, for example, in a perfectly inoffensive, innocuous manner something like:

"Hey, Dad."

"Yeah? What, Frank?"

"The toilet isn't flushing again. What do you say we hire a plumber, Dad?"

Then my father would come out of himself. *Then* he would say stuff. Oh, he would say lots of stuff.

Or else you could say something to him like:

"Hey, Dad."

"Yeah? What, Frank?"

"I just learned a new word today."

"What word?"

"Borborygmi."

"What does that mean?"

"It's the rumbling or the gurgling sound that your stomach makes when it's really gassy."

"Very good, Frank. That's a good word. That's an absolutely *amazing* word. Now that's precisely the kind of amazing word which those dictatorial Harvard muckety-mucks are always looking for in a high school senior."

"Are they really, Dad?"

"Oh, absolutely!"

And then my father would go back to reading the newspaper, or one of the many *Scientific American* magazines which he was forever bringing home with him from the office.

***

One evening at the beginning of December, however, even my generally taciturn and remote father succumbed to the corrosive effects of AGITATION. We were sitting down at the dinner table—eating dinner of course (in virtual silence)—when all of a sudden Dad blurted out:

"You know, there's a lot more to life, son, than just sitting around on your ass, vegetating."

"Vegetating, huh?"

"Yeah. You know.... Moping around. Being a sad sack."

I didn't know exactly how to respond to this obviously provocative and loaded comment, so I didn't try to. I just sat there. Sometimes you have to do that. You have to give generally taciturn, reserved people an extremely generous, wide berth when they finally decide to start venting their spleens. Otherwise—who knows? You might end up with a black eye.

My father addressed me yet again at that point—which was even more mysterious and disconcerting. It was like a second miracle on top of the first miracle. A royal flush right after a straight one. He said to me:

"I don't want you moping around here, being a sad sack, any longer, Frank. Is that clear?"

"Yeah. Sure, Dad."

"DO SOMETHING."

"Like what?"

"How the hell should I know? What—do I look like a guidance counselor to you or something?"

"No. Not exactly, Dad."

"How about a psychiatrist?"

"No, Dad. You don't look like a psychiatrist either."

At that point my father muttered something. It sounded a lot like "I hate psychiatrists" or "I loathe psychiatrists. They're even worse that those fucking plumbers are." But I could be wrong about this. I could be dead wrong. After all, my father rarely used the word "fucking" unless he was extremely agitated by the world's cupidity.

Then he said to me right after he'd finished his muttering—which may or may not have included an expletive concerning The Plumbing Profession.... He said to me: "What you do with the rest of your life, kid, is *your* problem. It ain't *my* problem. But I gotta tell you, sonny boy—just between you, me, your mother, and the lamp post—I am getting REALLY REALLY REALLY TIRED of this 'helpless and hopeless' sad sack routine of yours." My father slammed his fist down on the table hard then—extremely violently—like he was trying to kill it. The knives jumped. The plates clattered. The baked potatoes fell onto the kitchen floor and started rolling around under the table stupidly. My father got down on his hands and knees then and began picking them up. It was pretty pathetic.

Then he picked up a nice big one—a nice big fat ugly dimpled one—baked to perfection until the skin was crispy—and then he threw it at me just as violently.

That did it. Dinner was over. I withdrew to The Bastion and immediately consulted my journal....

***

Safe and sound once again within the spiritually restorative, salubrious environment of my own unadorned, simple bedroom; whose powder blue cerulean walls and whose powder blue cerulean ceiling seemed to make its restorative and salubrious properties even more restorative and even more salubrious—safe and sounds within the calming room, I say, I began reviewing with commensurate calmness the day's tumultuous and unsettling events. And then the week's tumultuous and unsettling events. And then the month's. And then the autumn's—after I had returned home—the conquering hero—from my absurdly costly "Ivory Tower Campaign." Overall, it had been a shitty autumn. Several days after the Labor Day weekend, for example, I received a very strange and unusual phone call from a person claiming to be my mother's cardiologist.

"Is this Franklin Horatio Archibald Cohen?" inquired the person claiming to be the cardiologist.

"It is. Who's this?"

"This is Dr. Seymour Ellenbogen speaking, Franklin, and I would very much like to talk with you."

"To talk with *me*, huh?"

"That's right."

"Do I know you?"

"No. You don't know me. But your mother knows me. I'm her cardiologist."

"I didn't know my mother had a cardiologist."

"Well, she does, Frank. And I'm it."

At that point I was expecting this Dr. Ellenbogen to break the news to me that my mother was ill. That she had an approximately 99% occlusion of every single one of her coronary arteries and that she immediately needed to have a heart transplant—only that she was too senile to make an informed decision about it. I mean… why else would a cardiologist want to speak to a family member and not to the patient directly?

Bracing myself, therefore—in light of this eminently logical and rational conclusion—for something really dire and probably terminal, I said then to this Dr. Ellenbogen:

"Okay, Doc. Let 'er rip. What exactly is wrong with my mother?"

"Wrong with her?"

"Yeah."

"Nothing. Nothing is wrong with her. She's perfectly fine, Frank."

"Then what do you want to talk to me for?"

"Because she asked me to."

"Because she *asked* you to?"

"Yes, that's right, Frank. As a personal favor to her."

"Well, what on earth would she do that for?"

At that point Dr. Ellenbogen—I mean, Good Samaritan Dr. Ellenbogen—explained to me why she had asked him to call me.

"Your mother," he said, "thinks you're depressed."

"Oh she does, does she?"

"Yes. That's right, Frank. She's very worried about you. Talks about you all the time."

"And you believe her?"

"Believe what, Frank?"

"That I'm 'depressed.'"

"Well, I don't know what to believe."

"What kind of a doctor did you say you were again? A psychiatrist?"

"No. A cardiologist."

"Well then, seeing as how A) you're not a psychiatrist, Doctor; and B) you yourself have just admitted that you have absolutely no fucking idea what to make of these inane ramblings; why in God's name didn't you just refer Ma to a good therapist?"

"Well, your mother isn't the one who's depressed, Frank."

"Well, who is then?"

"She says you are."

"Who cares what *she* says? She's a sick woman. A *diseased* woman."

"Well, about that...."

"Yeah, what about it?"

"Have you been having any strange thoughts lately?"

"What are you talking about?"

"You know.... *Dark* thoughts?"

"I don't believe this!"

"Believe what, Frank?"

"That I'm still pissing away my valuable time talking to some Friar Laurence with a medical license."

"Well.... I mean if we can't even begin to scratch *the surface*, Franklin...."

"HEY, WHY DON'T YOU GO SCRATCH YOUR ASSHOLE, SEYMOUR!"

At that point I slammed the phone down.

***

The next morning my mother said to me:

"What the hell did you say to Dr. Ellenbogen?"

"Who the fuck is Dr. Ellenbogen?"

"Don't give me that shit," she said. "He said you were extremely rude and disrespectful to him."

"Define 'extremely rude and disrespectful.'"

"He said you called him Seymour and told him to go scratch his asshole."

"Did I?" I said. "I don't remember."

"You told my cardiologist to go scratch his asshole?"

"If you say so," I said.

"What—are you retarded or something?"

"Am I retarded? Am *I* retarded? Talk about the pot calling the kettle black!"

"Well, what the hell does that mean?"

"It means what gives you the right to tell some asshole doctor that you think I'm depressed?"

"Well, you are depressed."

"No, I'm not depressed! But even if I was depressed, what gives you the right?"

"Well, he is a doctor, you know."

"That's not the point, Ma."

"Well, what is the point, Frank?"

"The point is that you can't do that."

"Well, why can't I?"

"Because it's... sick."

"Well, what do you mean by sick, Frank?"

"I mean it's not right. It's inappropriate."

"Inappropriate?"

"That's right."

"But how *exactly* is it inappropriate?"

My mother didn't understand this. I mean... she certainly knew what the word "inappropriate" meant, but she just couldn't quite seem to wrap her head around the *actual* meaning behind the literal one. It was like trying to explain to some horny teenager that you can't just randomly approach girls at the mall and ask 'em point blank if they want to fuck—at least not if you're serious about getting laid, that is. Maybe Ellenbogen could explain it to her. After all, Ellenbogen was her cardiologist. And if your cardiologist can't explain it to you, then who can, right? I'm being facetious here.

***

So then. Just to summarize: On the one hand, my demented mother was running around all over fucking Manhattan, making office appointments with every physician who she'd ever consulted over the past decade—with every cardiologist; with every rheumatologist; with every gynecologist; with every podiatrist even—telling them all that her son was depressed. While, on the other hand, my demented father—an impeccably moral & just man who lit votive candles on Friday evenings in strict observance of the Jewish Sabbath—in a fit of blind, uncontrollable fury or perhaps unresolved psychosexual rage, had just attempted to assassinate me—his youngest adorable, genius offspring—using, as an impromptu weapon, a delicious Idaho baked potato. Something had to give—obviously. Either I had to give. Or they had to give. Or all of us had to give. Or none of us had to give. And seeing as how it wasn't terribly likely that anybody was going to be giving anything at any time in the foreseeable future, I decided on one particularly dismal day of that particularly dismal autumn of which I speak—being a cool, calculating, detached realist as well as a dewy-eyed, impractical dreamer—to start considering all of my various options. I mean... to *seriously* start considering them without my usual & customary insouciant veneer.

Now, one of these various options (obviously) would have been to do exactly what my parents had wanted me to do; that is to say, to bite the bullet and to take the courses. Could I do it? Yes. Of course I could do it. I mean, I could do lots of things which I found repugnant—and it wasn't even *that* repugnant. I mean... compared to fighting, say, in Vietnam or something. Fighting, say, in Vietnam or something would have been a heck of a lot more repugnant than taking a couple of lousy Pre-Med Science courses. So that was the first option at my disposal, anyway: The Appeasement Option. The Acquiescence Option. The Surrender Option. The Chicken Option. Still another option would have been to "abandon ship"—to find a minimum wage-paying clerical job in some soul-less cubicle in the bowels of Manhattan; while at the same time living in a tiny apartment with three or four other losers—I mean, Liberal Arts English Majors. Still a third option would have been to blow my brains out. Spatter my extremely superior adorable gray matter all over Ma's Persian carpet with Mr. Wertheimer's trusty .45. That would teach Ma a lesson alright—teach her not to fuck around with The Adorable Genius. The only problem with that option, however, was that.... Well.... You know.... That really wasn't such a smart option. What I *should* have done was go with the second option. I know that now of course. But I didn't then. Instead of going with the second option—which, by the way, wouldn't have been such a great option either—I went with the first option—i.e., The Appeasement Option— rationalizing this stupid decision of mine by telling myself that it was really a smart decision. A shrewd decision. An eminently reasonable and oh-so-clever decision. I mean... just what exactly was so terrible about registering for a few Science courses? Simply registering for a few Science courses wasn't exactly going to kill me, right? Right! As a matter of fact, it might even help me. It might even turn out to be a colossal Godsend. I mean... it would serve to placate The Two Swamp Creatures while at the same time buying me a free ticket out of that depressing "Palookaville" known as The Bronx. And while I was there, by the way—on the exciting Isle of Manhattan—impersonating a fine, upstanding, idealistic lad who wanted nothing more than to become a doctor; I could go to The Guggenheim and to The Metropolitan. Hang out at The Strand Bookstore. Drink cappuccinos until I was blue in the face at The Caffe Reggio down on MacDougal Street. Now that wouldn't be so bad, would it? The Caffe Reggio would be my first stop just as soon as I had gotten off of the #6 train. I'd get a nice table under the awning where I would sit peacefully and contentedly, savoring my freshly-brewed caffeinated beverage while engaging in all sorts of splendid fantasies about my future novels, my future stories, my future poems, my future essays. Yes.... It would be one big *dolce far niente* for Franklin Cohen, that sly impersonator.

And so stupidly—so stupidly—so very very very stupidly—I selected Door #1 instead of Door #2, which would obviously have been a better door if only I had been a wiser person. But no matter. No matter. In the end, it really didn't make a bit of difference. In the end I was still able to find my way to that one, special, unique place which Fate had reserved just for me. It just took me a little longer to finally get there. That's all. But I still got there. I still got there! You choose one door instead of another door and you think you've chosen the wrong door. But you really haven't. It's the right door! No matter which one you choose, it's still the right one.

3. YOU CAN LEAD A HORSE TO WATER BUT YOU CAN'T MAKE IT DRINK

To be perfectly honest about Organic Chemistry—or "Introductory Organic Chemistry"—or "Pre-Med Organic Chemistry"—or "that motherfucking Organic Chemistry course" as it was very commonly and very lovingly referred to by its most enthusiastic and ardent admirers—it was, to say the very least, an unmitigated, colossal disaster. It was not at all like Social Psychology. It was not at all like Political Science. It bore no resemblance whatsoever to Art History, or to Modern Poetry, or to "Dostoyevsky For Free Spirits," or to "The Collective Unconsciousness In German Expressionism," or to "Jean-Luc Godard And The New Wave In French Cinema." The thing was a bitch. It was incredibly difficult. I mean... really, really, really *difficult*. The Marquis de Sade would have loved taking this course. It would have been right up his alley. As a matter of fact, I think he did take it. I mean... that certainly would have explained everything, right? The total and complete immersion in every conceivable type of criminal debauchery; while at the same being chronicled in the coolest and most baroque of styles—clearly one of the manifestations of an erstwhile Organic Chemistry student. And the same would go for Henry Miller. This guy *also* probably took the course just before writing *Tropic Of Cancer*. I mean... how else do you explain Miller's annoying, if not downright infuriating, name-dropping all throughout this meandering novel—jam-packed with its incessant references to various novelists, various poets, various painters, various sculptors, various composers, various philosophers—not that Miller has anything particularly insightful to say about any of them, mind you. It's just *name-dropping* for the sake of name-dropping; showing off for the sake of showing off. Anyway... note Miller's ostentatious, sophomoric name-dropping, and then—right after you've finished noting it—pick up a copy of _Organic Chemistry_ by those two lovable funsters, Morrison & Boyd, and see what it does to you—how it "rearranges" your intellectual, psychological, moral and molecular structures. Do you follow my drift? Am I being too subtle here? No. I don't think so. I don't think I'm being too subtle here. After all, I _am_ a genius, right? An _adorable_ genius? An _irrepressible_ genius? And—as we all know—all such geniuses of the adorable, irrepressible variety are supposed to be subtle, are _expected_ to be subtle. So I'm just being what I should be. I'm just being true to my nature—to my inherently subtle, irrepressibly adorable nature. So cut me a little slack, will you? Just read between the lines, will you? Nine tenths of all icebergs are hidden beneath the water's surface. Well, the same thing goes for books, right? At least for _good_ books. At least for subtle ones. Ten percent "above the water"—ninety percent "below the water." Now... I don't know whether this is a good book or whether it's a really lousy one. But I'm trying, Reader. I'm really trying. Respect me and I'll respect you. Don't underestimate me, and I won't underestimate you. Give me _your_ best, and I'll give you _my_ best.

Greater love hath no author.

Anyway.... The point is that if even The Genius—The _Adorable_ Genius—couldn't make head nor tail out of this Morrison & Boyd mishmosh, then who could? Who _could?_ Riddle me that, my subtle readers! True: It wasn't _total_ jibberish. I mean... not at first it wasn't anyway. They started you off sanely enough; with a few eminently reasonable, lucid concepts. Something about atoms and protons and neutrons and electrons; but then, somewhere along the line—very slyly—very subtly—very deviously—very _sadistically_— sooner than you were able to say: "Holy shit! This is complicated. I mean, this is _really really really_ complicated. What the hell have I gotten myself into? Give me my money back, you fucking sadists!"—they started speeding things up BIG TIME. They started bombarding you with all of this... STUFF—with all of these terribly complicated, nasty THEORIES. From the very beginning I knew it was hopeless—although I certainly put up a brave front. I saw a hurdle—I jumped over the hurdle; or, rather, I _tried_ *valiantly* to jump over the hurdle, only to realize a moment later that the damned hurdle was too high to clear! Even the tiny ones—the introductory ones—*the teensy-weensy, little baby ones*—were too high for The Adorable Genius! I wasn't a jumper; I was a dreamer. I didn't jump high; I dreamed high—which was a perfectly respectable and admirable quality to have if you were one of those dewy-eyed, sensitive English majors who preferred *The Appassionata* to *Stairway To Heaven*, and *The Genealogy Of Morals* to *Love Story*. But if you thought that listening to a little Beethoven or cozying up to a little Nietzsche was going to get you an A minus in Organic Chemistry, boy, were you in for a surprise, buster. Oh, it was going to be beautiful—just beautiful—that stunned, bewildered, vacant look in your eyes when you suddenly realized that you were no longer in Kansas.

My mother—who immediately freaked out at my clearly pathetic attempts at successful hurdle-jumping—promptly procured the services of a tutor. Some Swedish or Norwegian twit by the name of "Ragnar" or "Ragnor." "Ragnar"—or "Ragnor"—didn't just tutor me, mind you. He tutored seven other adorable geniuses simultaneously in the school library. We all sat around a big conference table with old Ragnar—or Ragnor—presiding over it like The Pope; and then old Ragnar—or Ragnor—would start yapping away about carbon molecules—about how cute they were; about how logical they were—with an accent as thick as molasses.

There was a girl who sat next to me in these tutoring sessions with old Ragnar. The girl's name was Beverly. Beverly Feingold. Beverly was like me. Beverly wasn't what you'd call a "Science" person. In fact, she was just the opposite of what you'd call a "Science" person. She was what you'd call an "Anti-Science" or a "Science-Allergic" person— meaning that both of us experienced severe allergic reactions whenever we came into contact with you know what.

Sometimes my "mirror image" and I would have these very interesting scientific discussions. We would talk occasionally after class about the Almighty, All-Knowing, All-Seeing, Dreaded Carbon Atom;

which both of us were pretty sure wasn't so much the building block of all organic matter; as it was an eight-inch-long dildo which was being continually shoved up our butt cheeks. I would open up "The Big O. C. Book" during these celebrated "discussions" of ours—that amazingly gratuitous and sadistic tome which Beverly's parents, as well as my own parents, had willingly shelled out over a hundred dollars for—and then I would point to some page—to some cute, little, sadistic molecule or something. And then I would say to my "mirror image' in an exceedingly hurt, wounded, indignant voice:

"Hey, Beverly...."

"Yes, Franklin?"

"Do you understand any of this stuff? I mean... do you really know what they hell they're talking about here?"

"No, Frank. I don't."

Beverly—if nothing else—was always extremely forthcoming and extremely direct when it came to acknowledging her complete ignorance in matters both scientific as well as un-scientific. She was an impeccably honest and sincere dummy—just like I was. I'll give her that much.

"I think it means that the first one is a hydrogen atom. And that it binds with the second one—which is an oxygen atom. And that they're both looking to attract the attention of this... this... this fuzzy thing."

"Fuzzy thing?"

"You know. This electron."

"Oh."

"But, Jesus, Franklin. I don't know. You're asking the wrong person. It's all Greek to me."

"Yeah. Me, too. It's like a brick wall. I get a migraine every time I see this shit."

"Well, then why don't you ask Ragnar about it? I mean... we're certainly paying the guy enough money, aren't we?"

"Fuck Ragnar," I said to Beverly. "I can't understand a word he says with that Scandinavian meatball accent of his."

"Well, why don't you ask Shelley then?" Shelley was this Orthodox

Jewish girl who was also in our Organic Chemistry class. Shelley was no dunce. Shelley was brilliant—a real math whiz. Shelley didn't need a Ragnar. She needed a boyfriend—to go to *schule* with.

"I don't think so," I said to Beverly.

"Why not?"

"Because she's got this crush on me. That's why. Because she's *in love* with me—can't live without me. I'm afraid if I ask her for help, she's gonna interpret it as a marriage proposal."

Beverly chuckled.

"No, I'm serious, Bev. You see the way she follows me around everywhere? With those sad, puppy dog eyes of hers?"

"She does not."

"She does too. She wants a boyfriend *real bad*. I know it—you know it."

"So what's wrong with wanting a boyfriend?"

"Nothing's wrong with it."

"So what's the problem then?"

"The problem," I said to Beverly, "is that her desperation is like battery acid. Every time I run into Shelley, it's like... WOULD JA PLEEEEEZE BE MY BOYFRIEND, FRANKLIN? WOULD JA? WOULD JA? WOULD JA? WOULD JA? Not exactly my type of battery acid."

"And just what exactly is your type of 'battery acid'?"

"You are, my little angel. Your battery acid is my ambrosia."

"What's ambrosia?"

"It's like honey."

"Oh."

Beverly thought about it for a couple of seconds—trying to decide, I guess, whether I was hitting on her.

"Are you hitting on me?" Beverly asked me.

"No, Beverly. I'm not hitting on you."

Then I said to Beverly, changing the subject now:

"So... what are your big plans for the weekend, my dear?"

"Oh... I think I'm gonna get wasted at this party on Saturday."

"Oh, really? Where at?"

"Bleecker Street. Around seven-ish. My sister's boyfriend just graduated from NYU Film School, so they're having this little thing-ee for him. You want to come along, Frank?"

"No, thanks."

"Aw, come on, Frank. It'll be fun."

"Nah, that's okay, Beverly. I hate parties—*loathe* parties."

"What's the problem, Frank?"

"No problem."

"What—you afraid you'll run into Shelley there?"

"Very funny, Bev. Yeah. A little bit."

Beverly chuckled again. So did I. There was something about old Beverly that I really liked. That I found... well... charming. At the same time, however, I *didn't* like it. I found it cloying somehow. And it kind of repulsed me. I often feel that way when I'm around humans. First comes The Novelty Phase; first comes The Charm Phase. And then comes The Repulsion Phase; The "Oh, shit! Not another one!" Phase. Not to worry, however. For the time being it was all good. Beverly Feingold was a Science Retard, and Franklin Cohen was also a Science Retard. And somehow—some way—amid the storm-tossed, chaotic Seas Of Life—we had managed to find each other—the two Science Retards. Sometimes, I swear, there is more to life than meets the eye.

As Beverly started walking away from me—back to her studio apartment on West 11th Street—I took a good, long, hard look at her. Beverly Feingold was a large woman. She wasn't really *fat*, mind you. Just large. With big hips and big thighs and big calves and pendulous breasts. Someday, I thought to myself, when you give birth to your first child, Beverly, you will blow up like Texas. Like Idaho. Like Missouri. Women like Beverly were susceptible to great weight changes, their metabolisms being notoriously fickle. Beverly would gain *much* weight in the ensuing child-rearing wonder years; and as a result of that gained weight and that veritable Atlantic Ocean of dirty diapers—some disposable; some non-disposable; some from Walmart; some from K-Mart; some from a service, perhaps, specializing in diapers made out of only the finest hypoallergenic cotton.... In those ensuing child-rearing wonder years, I say, that motherfucking Organic Chemistry textbook, which was now turning out to be such a horrific nightmare for us Science geniuses, would end up in due course at some yard sale in Mamaroneck. Or in Larchmont. Or in Yorktown Heights. Or in Mount Kisco. Or in Chappaqua. Which nobody would even notice—let alone consider buying for a lousy buck or two.

***

Later that evening, about an hour or so after supper, while I was lying comfortably on my twin mattress staring up at the pale blue stucco ceiling, trying my damnedest to figure out just why the hell it was exactly that The Good Lord, in His infinite wisdom, had decided to fashion me into the shape of a human—as opposed to, say, into the shape of a dog; or a cat; or cockroach; or a lollipop; or a cloud; or an asteroid; or a pencil; or a piece of lint—I was lying comfortably on my twin mattress, I say, trying my damnedest to solve The Eternal Conundrum; when all of a sudden I got a phone call from that other Mathematical & Scientific Whiz Kid, not to mention future gynecologist or cardiologist, or future gynecologist *and* cardiologist—one Beverly "The Brain" Feingold.

Big Beverly was fucked up. She was extremely fucked up. There was a decidedly far-away, euphoric quality to Beverly Feingold's Bleecker Street "party voice" which I immediately picked up on. The euphoria, no doubt, was due to the lop-sided, screwy effects of a combination of rot-gut hard liquor—such as Tequila maybe, or straight scotch—and some kind of mind-altering, potent hallucinogen. I couldn't quite put my finger on the specific hallucinogen which Beverly had ingested of course—not being a mind reader—but I did recall Beverly mentioning to me on more than just a few occasions that her sister Karen liked dropping acid—so I naturally assumed that it was acid. Either acid or maybe mescaline. Or maybe quaaludes. Or strong hash.

Beverly's sister, evidently, was into to all sorts of chemical substances.

"Hello, Frank?" said Euphoric Beverly.

"Yeah. Hi, Beverly. How's it going, girl?"

"Oh, it's going great, Franklin. Just great. I feel like I'm floating on a baked potato."

"Acid or mescaline?" I said to Beverly at that point.

"What?"

"Acid or mescaline?" I said to Beverly once more.

"What?"

"ACID OR MESCALINE. ARE YOU ON ACID OR ARE YOU ON MESCALINE, BEVERLY?"

"Neither," said Beverly.

"Well, what are you on then?"

"Uh...Valium."

Yes. Of course. Good old Valium. I had forgotten about good old Valium. When in doubt, stick to The Classics. None of this "mind-altering" psychedelic shit.

At that point Beverly stopped talking. She suddenly "faded away" right after the Valium answer. Either we had been disconnected by the phone company or else she had dropped the phone in a drunken stupor. I cast my ballot for "the drunken stupor" candidate, seeing as how I could still hear all of the other "party animals" at this gala event yucking it up like there was no tomorrow. You know.... The latest disco music. Raucous laughter. The usual cacophony of human beings letting their hair down at social gatherings.

Then, all of a sudden, there was a loud scratching or dragging sound on the Bleecker Street end of the line, followed promptly by the words "dick weed!" Now, "dick weed!"—it should be noted at this point—was not an epithet which I had ever heard before. I had heard the term "asshole," of course. Pretty frequently. Almost daily, in fact. I mean... who hasn't heard that one? If you've never called anybody an "asshole" or been called an "asshole" yourself at least four or five times a week, then you really haven't lived much. You've been living what they call "a sheltered existence." Not to brag, but I know lots of epithets. I know: "Fuck Face." "Motherfucker." "Shit Head." "Ass Wipe." "Son of a Bitch." "Shit For Brains." "Cocksucker." "Douche Bag." "Wop." "Faggot." "Grease Ball." "Jew Boy." "Shylock." "Jungle Bunny." "Jerk Off." But never "Dick Weed." "Dick Weed" was an entirely new one—a novel epithet for annoying nit-wits. Ragnar—or Ragnor—was probably a "dick week," for example. My friend Bill from the old neighborhood, whose father was now an insurance actuary, was also probably a "dick weed." People, in general, who thought that they knew things, but who really didn't—and who never would—were definitely gigantic "dick weeds." The world was full of such gigantic "dick weeds." They were the experts. They were the authorities. They were the gurus. They were the critics. I didn't really care very much for critics. I thought that critics were just basically weaklings—too cowardly to press on after they had gotten their first real whiff of failure. Ditto for the so-called "gurus." Any guru really worth his weight in salt kept his mouth shut and his eyes open.

"Hello, Frank?"

"Yeah. Hi, Beverly."

"Gee. I'm really sorry about that, Franklin. I dropped the phone on the fucking floor. Some dick weed tried to grab it from me."

"I hear you, girl," I said to Beverly. "Just between you and me, baby doll, I've had just about all I can take of these motherfucking obnoxious dick weeks."

The phone dropped then for a second time. This time a man retrieved it.

"WHO'S THIS!" the man barked at me.

"WHO'S THIS!" I barked back at the man.

"WHO'S THIS!"

"NO. WHO'S THIS!"

"I ASKED YOU FIRST!"

"MOTHERFUCKING OBNOXIOUS DICK WEED!"

I slammed the handset down hard then, feeling terribly powerful and extremely pleased with myself.

Not bad, I thought. Not bad at all. Slamming phones down.... Giving orders.... Having people scurry about at your slightest whim.... It was all very tempting, wasn't it?

If only the awesome responsibility of trying to live up to my fullest potential—whether it was a great potential or whether it was a modest potential; whether it was an obvious potential or whether it was a latent one—hadn't weighed upon me quite so heavily, well.... Who knows? Who knows.... I could have really enjoyed this type of lifestyle.

About a minute later the phone rang again. What a shock. What a big shock.

"Hello, Frank?"

"Yeah, hi Beverly."

"How's it going, Frank?"

"It's going good, Beverly."

"What are you doing now?"

"Ah, nothing. What are you doing now?"

"Nothing either. Hey, Franklin?"

"Yeah, Beverly?"

"Can I ask you a question?"

"Yeah. Sure, Beverly."

"Do you like taking Organic Chemistry?"

"Yeah, sure I like taking Organic Chemistry. What's not to like about it?"

"No, really. Do you like taking it?"

"Yeah, sure. Like I like root canal."

"What?"

"I said almost as much as I like toe fungus."

Beverly started giggling at this point. She started giggling rather uncontrollably.

"It wasn't *that* funny," I said to Beverly.

"No, it was funny, Frank. You're very funny."

"Well, I think you're funny, too, Beverly. I think we're *both* funny. I think we're hilarious."

"What?" Beverly asked me again.

"I said we're two very, very funny people, Beverly."

"Nobody in Organic Chemistry has the least goddamned sense of humor. Not Ragnar. Not Shelley. Not Potato Head."

"Who's Potato Head?"

"You know—Potato Head. The bald guy who sits next to Shelley?"

"Oh, yeah. Right. You mean Eric."

"That's right. Eric—Mr. Potato Head. You're the only one, Frank. You're my super-hero."

"Gee. Thanks, Bev. That means a lot to me. Too bad my parents don't feel the same way about it."

"Feel the same way about what?"

"About my rapier-like, caustic wit."

"My parents are nice. But they're still dick weeds. They're *huge* dick weeds."

"Oh really?"

"Uh-huh."

"Say 'dick weed' again, would ja, Bev."

"...Like... whenever I'm around them they treat me like I'm a complete idiot. Like I'm a dork. A helpless baby. You know what I mean, Frank?"

"Uh-huh. I know exactly what you mean, Beverly."

"And they're always *giving* me stuff, too. Always *laying* all sorts of shit on me. Like.... 'Hey, sweetie pie, what do you say we get you this beautiful new stereo system because you really need a new stereo system' and 'Hey, bubala, what do you say we get you this beautiful new Toyota Corolla because your old one is really a death trap' and 'Don't worry about the abortion, sweetie, because Mommy and Daddy are gonna make all the arrangements. You just concentrate on feeling better about yourself—taking some courses, maybe. At NYU or something.'"

"Ah, Jesus...."

"Yeah. Exactly! And *then*—when they wanted me to register for this goddamned fucking chemistry course—"

The telephone dropped again. More scratching sounds and raucous laughter.

While I waited patiently—with bated breath—for the next Nobel laureate in Organic Chemistry to make her third sloppy, rambling phone call—for I just knew that it was going to be coming imminently—a third phone call—a third smudge—a third blotch—a third SPLAT!— originating from some tenement building in the heart of Greenwich Village where the dope was plentiful.... As I waited, I say, for my "mirror image" to make her third sloppy, rambling phone call, I proceeded to distract myself in the intervening "down" time by inspecting my fingernails extremely carefully. With literally painstaking, meticulous precision. What strange, shell-like structures they were, I thought—these shiny, indurate "fingernails" of mine. What peculiar features they had! What bizarre attributes! Why, it was almost as if I had never seen them before. I mean, *really* seen them. Appreciated their "weirdness." Son of a gun! I had "fingernails!" I had these strange "shells" on the tips of my fingers—like the shells on a shrimp, maybe. Like the scales on a reptile—some deadly rattlesnake or disgusting iguana. And stranger still, there were these weird "markings" on them— these tiny ridges or subtle vertical bands running all along their entire length. What was up with that? I wondered. I mean, what the heck did that mean—the fact that I had these "tiny ridges" or "subtle vertical bands" running all along the length of the shells? Was it a good thing? Was it a bad thing? Was it a normal thing? Was it a *healthy* thing? Somewhere—a long time ago—I had read something about this anomaly. Something to the effect that such "tiny ridges" or "subtle vertical bands" could be symptomatic of a larger problem. Of an internal— maybe even a fatal—problem. Ah jeez, I thought to myself. Does it never end? Must it always rankle? Every second of every day worrying about heart disease. Liver disease. Lou Gehrig's Disease.

Cancer. Thank God for *The Merck Manual*. *The Merck Manual* was my Old Testament. My rod and my staff. My cup that runneth over. *The Merck Manual* would prepare a table before me in the presence of mine enemies. And I would be protected from disgusting diseases. Like Lou Gehrig's Disease. Like Gonorrhea....

"—And *then*—when they finally took the gloves off and decided to show me their true colors—"

"When *who* finally took the gloves off and decided to show you their true colors, Beverly?"

"Why, my parents of course, you silly goose!"

"Oh, yeah. Right. The two dick weeds...."

"—they said to me: 'Listen, bubala. Here's the deal: If you don't register for this fucking chemistry course and do it *gratefully*—without a big chip on your shoulder—then you can forget about ever seeing Maryanne again.'"

"Who the fuck is Maryanne?"

"She's my therapist."

"Oh, right. The therapist. I should have known that. Okay. Continue."

"—I said to them: 'Listen, you guys. I don't want to become a gynecologist. Let Karen become the gynecologist. She's smart. She likes Math. She won all of those Science prizes. I don't want to take Organic Chemistry. Why should *I* have to become the doctor?'"

"Absolutely goddamn one hundred percent fucking right, Beverly!" I responded to Beverly's excessive whining with as much enthusiasm as I was able to muster. "The nerve of those two dick weeds! Who the hell are those two dick weeds to start threatening you with ultimatums! Blackmailing you emotionally—and using Maryanne of all people!"

"Exactly, Franklin!"

"Exactly, Beverly!"

I was very quickly losing interest in the Greek tragedy which was Beverly Feingold. Beverly Feingold was a rambling Valium abuser. She was a rambling Valium abuser and she was also a whiny Valium abuser.

In addition to this, she was also big-boned. With big, sloppy, rambling breasts. I thought of those big bones of hers. Those big, sloppy, rambling breasts of hers. Those cellulite-laced buttocks of hers. That fertile pelvis of hers. That pubic hair of hers. Missouri. Montana. Nevada. _Nebraska_....

The phone dropped yet again. Wonder of wonders! Miracle of miracles! I sat there—hardly breathing at all—and then I braced myself for the next phone call. Which eventually came, of course. As did a fifth phone call. And then a sixth phone call. And then a seventh phone call. Etcetera, etcetera. All in all, I think there were ten phone calls—ten sloppy, rambling SPLATS!—although I could be wrong about this. There could have been more than ten. There could have been eleven. There could have been twelve. There could have been thirteen. Hell. There could have been twenty, even. What the hell was the fucking difference? I mean, after the first sloppy, rambling phone call, it was just more of the same shit anyway, wasn't it? No highs—no lows. No peaks—no valleys. No twists—no turns. No curve balls—no anything. Some way of making a phone call, huh? Not exactly my way of making a phone call—or, for that matter, of telling a story. If that's the way you're planning on telling a story to someone—without any peaks and without any valleys; without any highs and without any lows; without any twists and without any turns; without any curve balls; without any anything—then you might as well not tell it at all because nobody with any intelligence is going to want to hear it. You're going to bore them.

***

As dumb luck would have it, I never actually received the F or the F minus which I so richly deserved in this cruelest, most sadistic, most gratuitously blistering of all obstacle courses. I got a C minus instead—a miraculous C minus. My Organic Chemistry professor—an emaciated-looking English dude whose crystal clear blue eyes, wrinkled brow, and hooked nose made him look exactly like a common buzzard—told me straight to my face what a big, big disappointment I was. "Cohen," lamented Professor Quigley, "I have a heavy, heavy, *heavy* heart. You took so many meticulous notes. You had so much *curiosity*. What happened to you, dear boy? I don't understand it. You just... *wilted!*"

"Oh, I wilted alright," I was just a hair's breadth away from saying to Quigley, "because you, sir, are to The Teaching Profession what boll weevils are to Agriculture. That's the reason why I 'wilted,' asshole!"

Obviously, I didn't say that. It was beyond that. Way beyond it. If I had really wanted to start squabbling with every "Professor Quigley" who ever crossed my path, then there would have been no end to all of the squabbling. My entire life would have consisted of nothing but squabbling—which is not exactly the way to go, I think, if you're planning on living what's known as "The Examined Life;" an essential component of which is the almost religious avoidance of any "Examined Life"-distracting altercations. My head bent in pretend shame, trying to look as penitent as a convicted child molester being re-released into polite society, I just stared silently at my Adidas sneakers—which had been a pristine, dazzling white when I had first purchased them at *The Sports Authority*; but which were now, after years of abuse, about as squeaky clean as a junky whore was.

***

Now: unless you're somebody who's been in a coma for the last sixty-five or seventy pages, you will have no doubt observed that all of my thoughts and all of my perceptions regarding The General Field known as SCIENCE have so far been pretty negative. I won't deny this. They've been abysmal—but abysmal, you understand, not because there was anything inherently abysmal about studying carbon-based molecular compounds; or about studying the process by which green plants used the energy of sunlight to produce oxygen; but, rather (and this is the crucial part) *because I myself was such an abysmal student!* I had neither the aptitude nor the inclination for exploring any of these scientific venues; and so—naturally—I regarded the lot of them (save for one very screwy, serendipitous exception) with the utmost displeasure. With *abysmal* displeasure.

What goes around, they say, comes around.

Garbage in, they say, garbage out.

Okay. So I hated Science. Always had hated it—always would hate it. I think we've pretty much sucked that lemon dry. Don't you? So let's move on now to another lemon, shall we?—to another big, fat, juicy, sour one in my veritable cornucopia of acrid courses. This lemon, however, was slightly different. It was an exceptional lemon—a *peculiar* lemon—insofar as it was not quite as disgustingly acrid as were all of the others in The Horn Of Plenty. I mean... I certainly don't want to give you the impression that I hated every single one of these Science courses. Because I didn't. I really didn't. I hated *most* of these Science courses but not *all* of these Science courses. I am not, after all, a hateful person by nature. I am a flexible person. I am a *judicious* person. When something is hateful, then—by God—I'll hate it. And when something is lovable, then—by God—I'll love it; although I do have to admit that— all things being considered—I have a far greater predilection for hating things than I do for loving them; seeing as how this farcical menagerie euphemistically called "The World" is not a particularly lovable—or even likeable—place.

Okay. So I hated Science. That is to say, I hated *most* Science. But Pre-Calculus, I didn't hate. I didn't love it, but I didn't hate it. You might say that I begrudgingly *tolerated it*—that I begrudgingly *endured it*—for the sake of my math teacher; who, as my "Big Eight" Pre-Med course load mechanically grinded on like a machinist's lathe and as my enthusiasm for it concomitantly wilted like an erect phallus in a Siberian winter, became... well... kind of a friend of mine. Actually, a very good friend. So I really had *two* friends during my "NYU Science Phase." I had Beverly "The Brain" Feingold, of course—my "main squeeze" during this perilous time—but now I also had Raymond "The *Real* Brain" Levashevsky, my Pre-Calculus math teacher. Beverly "The Brain"

Feingold was an extremely dull, boring, conventional person; whereas Raymond "The *Real* Brain" Levashevsky was an extremely unconventional, brilliant person. Beverly "The Brain" Feingold was probably going to end up by becoming a school teacher or a social worker—that is to say, once she had finally managed to get her shit together; whereas Raymond "The *Real* Brain" Levashevsky—being the extremely brilliant fellow that he was—was probably going to end up either by having a Medical Center named after him in honor of his towering achievements in the field of Math—you know... *The Raymond Levashevsky Hospital For Cancer And Allied Diseases...* or *The Raymond Levashevsky Institute For Rheumatological And Immune Disorders*— something like that, I mean; something REALLY BIG; or else he was going to end up by having a nervous breakdown and becoming a homeless person—you know... like one of those lost souls who you occasionally see in The City, wandering around Lower Manhattan pushing a shopping cart containing all of his worldly possessions.

Fate still hadn't quite decided yet just which exactly it was going to be for Raymond: fame or obscurity. A mahogany casket and a mausoleum, or a pine box in Potter's Field.

The future, as they say, was still wide open.

In any event, I loved Raymond. I loved Beverly, too, of course. That goes without saying. Only... what was Beverly's tepid, amateurish recital compared to Raymond's virtuoso, bravura performance; her nauseatingly predictable conventionality compared to Raymond's ostensibly social but actually reclusive nature? Obviously there was none. I mean, a comparison—a legitimate comparison. And so there you have it. Raymond triumphed. He triumphed overwhelmingly. Hail, Raymond! As you can well imagine, I've got a lot to say about him—this highly eccentric, mercurial Raymond character. I mean... hell. I've already pissed away—what?—ten pages?—thirteen pages?—fifteen pages?— describing Boring Beverly. So I guess that exceedingly slippery, mercurial Raymond deserves at the very least thirty pages of lucid prose, right? Thirty pages.... Forty pages.... Forty-five pages.... Or even fifty, maybe.

Fifty pages really isn't that much. Originally, it was around a hundred and twenty pages—until I finally came to my senses and decided to edit myself.

Anyway, here's what you need to know about this highly eccentric, mercurial math teacher:

1) He was obviously a fucking genius—or at least I think he was a fucking genius. I mean... who else but a fucking genius would have devoted the last eight and a half years of his life to proving conclusively in his dissertation—or at least he _claimed_ to have proved conclusively in his dissertation using a series of complex mathematical formulas—that the physical world doesn't really exist? Now... this to me is Genius Territory. Either Genius Territory or Flawed Genius Territory. Or both maybe. Probably both.

When I asked Raymond what the title of his eight-and-a-half-years-in-the-making, super-duper dissertation was, he just picked up the thing and threw it at me.

"Here you go," he said. "Eat your heart out."

"I can't read this," I immediately said to him.

"Well, why not?" he said.

"It's too long," I said.

"_Too long?_" he said.

"Yeah. It's too long," I said. "It's not really a title, Raymond."

"Well, what is it then?"

"It's a gorilla."

"Excuse me?"

"Here. Read it yourself."

Raymond read it then—I mean, he recited it then—since he already knew it by heart, being the author.

"Do you see what I mean?" I said.

"No. Not really," he said.

"Well, read it again then."

"No. _You_ read it!"

"Okay, okay. I'll _try_ to read it."

I tried to read it then—but I really couldn't. It was some interminably long, meandering hodge-podge of mathematical psychobabble like: *"The Illusion Of Physicality As A Spontaneous Post-Kantian / Hegelian Breakdown Of All A Priori Mathematical Models In The Context of Topological Supersymmetry In Which The Intrinsic Property Of All Stochastic Values And Differential Mathematical Formulas...."*

You get the idea, right? Psychobabble. Pure jibberish.

"You see what I mean, Ray?" I said to Raymond again.

Raymond didn't say anything, however. He just shrugged his shoulders as if he didn't give a shit.

"Now... if it were up to *me*—" I said to him at that point.

"Yeah, but it isn't up to you, now is it, slick?"

"—I'd call it *War And Math*," I said. "Or maybe I'd call it *Crime And Math*."

"*Crime And Math*, huh?"

"Yeah. It's good, right? I mean, it really rolls off of the old tongue just like butter 'n biscuits, don't it, Ray?"

Once again, Raymond didn't say anything.

That was the first—and the last—time that we ever spoke about his dissertation.

2) Raymond, like many people—that is to say, like many freakishly brilliant, exceptional people—eschewed the company of his own kind; preferring, instead, to be in the company of dunces. Now... I'm not going to get into a whole big thing here trying to explain to you just why this is exactly—that is to say, just why it is exactly that certain people—certain extremely talented, brilliant people—would rather socialize with extremely *dull* people instead of with other members of their own "elite" tribe. They just would. That's all. They're just like that. Some of them, anyway. As a matter of fact, I'm pretty sure that if you had confronted Raymond head on and specifically asked him why he had this "thing" for dunces, he would have looked at you as if you had had three heads. "What—*me?* Preferring the company of dunces? What are you talking

74

about? What dunces?" Brilliant people sometimes do that. They feign surprise. They appear bewildered—using bewilderment as a form of camouflage—just as the chameleon uses its own "camouflage" in order to blend in and to avoid detection. I mean... you can't just go around exuding dazzling brilliance all over the place, right? Rubbing it in peoples' faces—making them feel like fucking idiots—without there being certain... well... how shall I put it exactly? Certain... "undesirable, ill effects," shall we say? Certain... "unintended repercussions?" No. You really don't want to do that. You want to put a lid on all of the dazzling brilliance and just kind of "blend in" like our friend, the chameleon here, if you don't want to risk being eaten alive by some nasty snake or by some nasty lizard person.

Average people like average things. They mistrust brilliance. They are suspicious of brilliance. But it's not their fault really. They just don't know any better. They were just never taught any better. By real teachers. By *honest* teachers. When you've lived your entire life breathing nothing but foul air, it can be extremely upsetting being exposed to fresh air. Most people don't know how to handle it. They think it's dangerous. They think it's a trick. And then—when you try explaining to them that it's *not* dangerous and that it's *not* a trick—they kind of... *look* at you. Like you're a nut or something.

The true prisoner is his own jailer.

Anyway—whatever his motives might or might not have been—one thing was perfectly clear: Raymond "The Real Brain" Levashevsky gravitated towards dunces the way that vultures gravitated towards road kill. Being around them seemed to make him merry. To buoy his spirits. To fill some void. And so, naturally, he tended to seek them out with an uncommonly calculating and distinct robustness. For instance: There was this one particular low-life bar located on Eleventh Street & Broadway—right next to Ray's Famous Original Pizza—which Raymond absolutely loved going to. That was his main "ordinary people" hangout—the place, I mean, which he usually frequented in order to soak up "the healing vibes" of your everyday, average fuck up—your everyday, average wife beater, or child molester, or problem drinker, or commie agitator, or dope fiend, or petty drug dealer, or grifter, or ex-convict. I mean, the place was a real dive. A real shit hole. For losers. Maybe all of them weren't losers. Maybe some of them were actually "winners." You know.... Fine, upstanding, solid citizens with fine, upstanding, solid jobs—businessmen, plumbers, car mechanics, gym teachers—although I personally couldn't tell the difference between the child molesters and the gym teachers. I mean... to me they *all* looked like child molesters. Like wife beaters. Like drug addicts. Hey—wait a minute. Here's a thought: Maybe—*just maybe*—in reality they were all grad students!—all of these various malcontents and assorted dead beats. And maybe—*just maybe*—they had all just suddenly realized in the same terrifying and crushing moment that—yes indeed—it was quite true: they *still* had to pay back all of those astronomical student loans of theirs *in spite of the fact that they were all unemployed!* That would certainly have explained everything, wouldn't it? All of the dazed looks. All of the vacant stares. All of the blank expressions. All of the blunted affects....

Goodbye, Graduate School—Hello, Public Assistance.

Goodbye, Ivory Tower—Hello, Urban Jungle.

Goodbye, Sushi—Hello, McDonald's and Burger King.

Goodbye, Fair-Haired, Golden Dreams of becoming a Somebody in a world of nobodies—Hello, hard-edged, hellish reality of being nothing more than a soul-less statistic.

***

So anyway.... Just to recap.... Raymond Levashevsky—my exceedingly brilliant, eccentric math teacher—loved hanging out at this dive. At this gin mill. At this saloon. At this shit hole. As a matter of fact, we often used to call the place "The Shit Hole" or "The Shit House," or "Chez Merde"—which is French for "Shit House."

Now... for some dark, twisted, perverse reason, the obscure nature of which I can only hazard to guess at, Raymond Levashevsky—that chameleon-like, devious fellow—who used bewilderment as a form of subterfuge, and anonymity as a kind of sanctuary in a world populated by unscrupulous leeches—took a real shine to Franklin Cohen. Actually, I'm being slightly facetious here. The fact of the matter is that I knew *exactly* why he took a shine to me; just as I knew *exactly* why the same bad actors always seemed to end up playing all of the leading roles on The World Stage year after motherfucking year, decade after motherfucking decade; while so many truly deserving actors languished in complete obscurity. Why was that? I mean... why was it *really?* Why weren't all of these bad actors the ones who languished in complete obscurity? Why, after having been given more than ample opportunity to prove themselves, and having always failed abysmally to do so, hadn't they all been blacklisted—prohibited from ever acting again? Now that was *also* something which was worth writing about. It literally *cried out* to be written about. Actually, it already has been written about. Many times, in fact. By many authors. Only nobody reads them. *Nobody reads them!* Or if they do read them, then it means nothing to them. It's just an evening out. It's just a night's "entertainment." If Shakespeare had never existed, would the world *really* be any the poorer for it? I know we've all been *told* it would. We always have been. And we probably always will be. Nevertheless.... Nevertheless.... In spite of all of those fine, stirring, inspirational speeches and knee-jerk, rote responses to sincerely asked, probing questions—the world still rots. It still founders. It takes a strong person to endure the hypocrisy of it.

Anyway.... Back to Raymond. Yes, I understood very well why my eccentric math teacher had taken a shine to me; and—rest assured—it certainly didn't have anything to do with my literally non-existent mathematical prowess. I had already told Ray a few things about Ma— not *too* much—but enough apparently. Immediately Ray was hooked on Ma. From the very get-go. Right out of the starting gate. Ray found Ma enchanting, beguiling, intoxicating, bewitching, captivating, breath-taking, spellbinding... adorable. As a matter of fact, Ray found Ma *so* adorable and *so* intoxicating and *so* enchanting, etc., etc., so that even

Raymond—who was not exactly what I would have considered to be a shy person when it came to expressing his feelings—was rendered totally mute by Ma's... splendiferousness.

"You know, your mother is really something, Franklin." That was really all that he was capable of saying to me after I had finished describing to him one of our famous "sex talks."

"Yeah, tell me about it," I said to Raymond.

"She's like.... She's like.... She's kind of like...." Ray's voice trailed off at that point as he struggled to find the appropriate words. He couldn't, however. I couldn't either. We just sat there for a couple of seconds in complete silence—totally stumped. It was like we were looking out over the Pacific Ocean or something—trying to wrap our minds around its ineffable vastness. We couldn't, however. I mean, who can? *Who can?* I mean... the ocean is REALLY BIG, right? It's like... bigger than anything—except for the sky, maybe. And it isn't fucked up the way we humans are. It doesn't want to try to control everything. It doesn't want to try to explain everything. It doesn't want to try to kill everything that thinks differently from the way that *it* thinks. It's perfect. It's just perfect. It's everything we humans aren't. The moment passed then, and then Raymond said to me: "Hey, how about you and me get a little drinkee or two over at Geronimo's?" (Geronimo's—by the way—was the name of The Shit House before we started calling it "The Shit House"). I said to Ray: "Sure, Ray. Why not?" And then we went over there—to Geronimo's. We had a little drinkee or two there and we talked some more. Ray laughed a lot. He laughed incessantly. I laughed, too, of course—but not as much as Raymond did.

It was nice to find another person who found Ma so hysterically funny.

***

Eventually Ray introduced me to some of his drinking buddies at The Shit House. None of these people were particularly interesting. They simply drank there in order to kill time. Arielle was one of the time killers. Arielle was a butch lesbian. Arielle was also a cab driver who lived in a Single Room Occupancy hotel. Arielle would roll into The Shit House right after her shift ended—about 9 or 9:30—whereupon she would immediately start chain-smoking and ordering shots of Cutty Sark with beer chasers. Arielle was quite a drinker. She could drink any lesbian under the table. Wasn't very much of a talker, though. Almost never talked. *Hated* talking. And when she did talk, she always mumbled. She was always "Arielle, the butch mumbler"—the conveyor of dark, tragic, incestuous secrets. For instance: Arielle could be saying something as perfectly ordinary and as perfectly innocent as "Gee, fellas. Get this: This Cutty Sark and beer chaser is like... the best combo I've ever had! Why, I could drink a million of 'em without batting an eyelash"—only when it was Arielle who was the person saying it, it always sounded like some kind of shameful confession concerning her abusive childhood and her abusive parents, such as: "When I was eleven and a half years old my abusive father used to beat the shit out of me; while my abusive mother used to take pictures of it for the family album using her trusty Polaroid." Something like that, I mean. Something really... cringe-worthy. It was never: "Hi, fellas! I'm feeling really great today!" It was always: "Life is suffering. So why not just end it all?"

Not exactly the type of person who you wanted volunteering at your local Suicide Hot Line.

Raymond had another friend. Another member of "the inner sanctum." The guy's name was "The Smooch" or—less commonly—he was called "Smoochie." That's what everybody used to call him anyway, including Dorian, the sullen bartender—who was himself shit faced most of the time—as well as Isabella, the lone beer maid. Contrary to the rather rakish images, however, which The Smooch's moniker naturally conjured up, The Smooch was in no way, shape, or form an ostentatious, flamboyant "Ladies' Man," prone to constant public displays of physical affection. On the contrary. He was a loner—an extremely undemonstrative kind of person who seemed far beyond the usual physical urges which seem to tyrannize the rest of humanity. He was a tall, thin, lanky fellow—truly as skinny as a proverbial bean pole and without an ounce of fat on him anywhere. He had black hair which was always slicked back with some kind of heavy-duty pomade; was always unshaven—or at least always very badly shaven; wore faded blue jeans which were always ripped at the knees; aviator sunglasses; a black Harley-Davidson motorcycle jacket; and a profusion of imitation silver key chains perpetually hanging down from his leather belt. You know the look. We all know it. If I had a nickel for every time I've seen some conceited asshole in a Bowery gin mill sporting "The Smooch Look" and "The Smooch Attitude"— well… what can I tell you? I'd have a lot of nickels.

***

One night, the four of us were sitting together at The Shit House— drinking. We were drinking silently, as we would often do; our private thoughts being our true drinking buddies. I personally was thinking about Commander O'Brien, my immediate superior back on my home planet. Commander O'Brien was a good egg—not one to start throwing his weight around unless it became absolutely necessary to do so.

"Cohen," Commander O'Brien had said to me.

"Yes, Commander?" I had said to Commander O'Brien.

"Now…. Please bear in mind, Corporal…."

"Yes?"

"I can't actually *order* you to go to The Earth, to study the Earthlings in exquisite detail, and then—upon your return here—to become our leading authority on the subject."

"Yes, Sir. Whatever you say, Sir."

"As a matter of fact, Corporal Cohen…."

"Yes?"

"*Nobody* who we've sent to The Earth so far has ever come *even remotely close* to becoming a leading authority on these peculiar creatures."

"Nobody, Sir?"

"No. Nobody. So no pressure, my dear fellow! No need to worry, Corporal. Breathe easy. None of us here on Planet Malinla seriously expects you to crack these crazies. Just do the best that you can—no more, no less."

"Yes, Sir," I said to Commander O'Brien. "I will certainly give it my best shot, Sir."

"'At a boy!" said Commander O'Brien. "That's the spirit, Corporal! Semper fi!"

"Yes, Sir. Thank you, Sir."

"Oh—and another thing," said Commander O'Brien.

"Yes, Commander? What's the other thing?"

"Try to stay out of trouble, will you, Corporal? I mean, the last thing that The High Council needs is another embarrassing little *faux pas*."

"Yes, Sir! What do you mean, Sir?"

"Well, you remember what happened to Private Zog, don't you, Corporal?"

"Yes, Sir. That was most unfortunate."

Private Zog had been my immediate predecessor. Nice enough kind of guy, but just a bit of a shmuck—to be brutally honest about it. Zog started off like gangbusters—wrote some very insightful, informative pieces about what life was really like in Urban America. You know... massage parlors... prostitution... subway graffiti... fast food franchises... the usual postmodern commie bull shit declaring that individualism is passé, and that the only reason for creating art is to promote the latest flavor-of-the-month social cause. All of this was very impressive. The High Council—as you can well imagine—was exceedingly pleased with the quality of the Intel. But *then*, all of a sudden, with absolutely no warning whatsoever or official approval from The Home Office, Zog gets this crazy bug in his head that he's not just going to *observe* the humans (which—by the way—if I haven't already mentioned it—is like... the whole fucking point of the mission); but that he's actually going to try to *help* the humans by sharing with them just a tiny fraction of the vast stores of our accumulated knowledge. For instance: take this whole "Cure For Cancer Thing" which seems to have eluded the entire allopathic Medical Establishment since the inception of its so-called "War On Cancer." Well, Zog decides to share with humanity one of our simplest—not to mention TOTALLY FREE AND TOTALLY NON-TOXIC—remedies for this dreaded affliction; which is basically just a very common extract found in the deciduous vegetation of most carbon-based plant systems. Well.... No sooner has Zog let the proverbial "cat out of the bag," so to speak—first by being interviewed on a few "alternative media" radio stations; and then, in response to popular demand, by hosting his own radio show appropriately entitled *Cure Cancer Now And Forever!*—than The Federal Drug Administration, The American Medical Association, The American Cancer Society, The Centers for Disease Control, The National Institutes Of Health, The World Health Organization, and—lest we forget—The United States Department Of Justice Organized Crime And Racketeering Division all come down on Zog like a ton of bricks. After launching a merciless, non-stop, twenty-four-hour-a-day *ad hominem* attack on Zog—calling Zog "a slimy charlatan"—calling Zog "a snake oil salesman"—calling Zog "a barbaric witch doctor"—calling Zog "a Russian spy"—an FDA SWAT team eventually shows up at Zog's apartment building at 4 o'clock on a Sunday morning; whereupon Zog is spirited away, Nazi style, to an awaiting jail cell on Rikers Island. A speedy trial subsequently ensues—a "Kangaroo Court," I believe, is what you English-speaking humans would call it—followed by a stiff jail sentence in a maximum security penitentiary. Poor Zog. What a way to go, huh? Being shanked by his own cellmate over a pack of chewing gum. Fucking do-gooders....

Anyway.... There I am. I'm sitting together with my buddies—drinking—but I'm also secretly thinking about Do-Gooder Zog. I don't know what the others are thinking about. Maybe they're thinking about their own Private Zogs and their own Commander O'Briens—their own fact-finding, secret Earth missions. Raymond, I was pretty much convinced by now, was one such fellow star traveler; being far too sophisticated and far too subtle to have been the product of mere human parents. But the other two? I had my doubts. They just didn't look like the type—didn't *smell* like the type—who spent all of their spare alien, extra-terrestrial time hop-scotching from galaxy to galaxy, gathering valuable Intel for The Home Planet. Arielle confirms this when she suddenly breaks the silence. Arielle mumbles something—something dark. Another humiliating, grim confession, no doubt, taken from "The Arielle Family Archives." It sounded a lot like: "I started turning tricks for Mom and Dad right after I got my first menstrual period. But please don't ask me for any details because the whole experience was just too depressing." Raymond had to translate for me. He said: "Arielle says she wants to know how you got here tonight, Frank."

Okay. Fair enough.

"I drove here," I said to Arielle. "In my Dad's beautiful, new beige Chrysler."

"No shit, Frank," Raymond said to me then. "So your father's got a Chrysler, huh?"

"Yeah. A Newport," I said to Raymond.

"What year?"

"Sixty-seven."

"How much mileage on it?"

"Shit. I don't know."

"Gee. That's a mighty big car, Frank." That was The Smooch now, chiming in.

"Yeah, tell me about it. It's a monster. It burns gasoline like firewood, and you need like… half a block to park it properly. But that's okay. I really like it. There's nothing like driving an Army tank smack dab in the middle of a recession, right?"

"Yeah. Right, Frank. Absolutely!" That was The Smooch again, getting mildly animated. First time since I'd been introduced to the guy—he actually sounded like a human being. You know…. A real person. With real feelings. Somebody who actually gave a shit about something other than his stupid key chains.

"Hey, how about showing it to us, huh Frank?"

"What? The Army tank?"

"Duh…. Yeah the Army tank."

"Yeah, show us the Army tank, will you, Franklin?" That was Raymond again, also animated. "I bet your old man isn't exactly thrilled with the idea of your driving around in his precious chariot, is he?"

"Oh, he hates it like you wouldn't believe, Ray. Gives him stomach ulcers. Eats his heart out. He won't admit it of course, but it's as plain as day."

"I knew it!" exclaimed Raymond. "My father was exactly like that."

"My parents love anal sex," Arielle confessed to us at that point. "They just can't seem to get enough of it—but don't ask me for any details because I won't talk about it—I mean, I *can't* talk about it."

Nobody asked her for any details. God knows, we didn't want any. Arielle's shit was Arielle's shit. It wasn't our shit. We had our own shit. That's about the only thing I ever learned from drinking: Everybody's got their own shit, and it's just plain bad drinking etiquette to add your pile to somebody's else's pile.

Eventually Ray said to the crew: "Hey, what you say we split this gin mill?"

"Sounds good, Ray," I said to Raymond.

The Smooch concurred. So did The Mumbler.

And so we left the gin mill and started walking Uptown. We walked Uptown along Broadway for six blocks until we reached the Army tank.

The old Army tank, I should add at this point—what with its enormous girth and bright color—stuck out like a sore thumb on the otherwise deserted street. "Steal me. *Pleeeeeze.* STEAL ME! The guy who owns this car is a fucking idiot." That was basically what the Army tank was screaming to every car thief in the entire neighborhood.

I had to admit, it was pretty embarrassing.

"Wow. That's some nifty piece of junk you've got there," The Smooch said to me when he laid eyes on it.

"Yeah, ain't it a beauty? My father just had it simonized."

"Let's go for a ride, Frank."

"Yeah, let's go for a ride, Franklin."

"I have curly blond pubic hair which I am deeply deeply deeply ashamed of."

We all piled into the Chrysler then, extremely energized, and drove off.

***

We drove aimlessly for about twenty minutes. We drove Uptown. We drove Downtown. We drove East. We drove West. The Smooch wanted to take the wheel but I said to him: "Not on your fucking life, Smooch. You want to take the wheel—speak to my father first."

"Touchy," The Smooch said to me. "Very, very touchy, Franklin."

Then he wagged his finger at me.

Eventually we double parked at the *Dusk 'Til Dawn* liquor store, a charming little hole in the wall right next to The Port Authority Bus Terminal. Raymond—who had been sitting next to me—got out of the automobile to purchase the beer. I observed Raymond as he started to do this. I observed him carefully; I observed him *meticulously*. Dad, I think, would have been rather pleased with the way that I observed Raymond as he approached the liquor store—with the way that I observed the stately manner in which he moved, which was neither too hurried nor too slow; neither frenetic nor lackadaisical; but, rather, measured, resolute, unfaltering: extremely dignified. Finally, I thought to myself. *Finally.* At long last…. Hallelujah! A man who sees himself for what he really is. Who correctly recognizes his true worth, and who doesn't feel guilty about it or nauseatingly smug about it. Some people, you know…. Some people…. The way they carry themselves…. They walk like criminals—like hunted fugitives—afraid even to take a deep breath for fear of being arrested by the local authorities. And then, of course, you have your "worker bees"—your "slave laborers" and "beasts of burden"—who creep joylessly about the earth as if they were carrying hundred pound sacks of grain on their shoulders. No paid vacations for this crowd. No holidays. No sabbaticals. No respite. Just work! And then finally, you have your "special people"—your "big shots"—your "Royalty"—who carry themselves as if the world were beneath them, and as if they were doing the rest of us a huge favor by consenting to walk upon it—albeit begrudgingly. Not this singular spirit, however. Not this modern-day Spartan warrior whose every move seemed to exude AWARENESS and the concomitant readiness which goes along with AWARENESS. This Spartan was fully prepared to hold at Thermopylae for as long as it took. To fight the good fight. To fight the clean fight. To fight the virtuous fight. To fight *the noble* fight. And then—when the good clean virtuous noble fight became a fight no more, but merely an exercise in futility—to give the middle finger to the advancing Persian hordes and—by extension—to the entire universe.

No buffoonery.

No arrogance.

No false modesty.

No illusions.

A true Spartan. A *real* Spartan.

That was the impression that I got anyway—for what it's worth—as I observed Raymond.

Eventually Ray returned to the car—ah, but too soon, I thought. Too soon!—for I had wanted to observe "the true Spartan" for just a little longer, in his "martial" state. He returned—alas—and then he said to The Smooch: "Here, Rockefeller. Take this."—and then he dumped the two six packs and jug of dago red onto The Smooch's lap. The Smooch groaned a little and then Raymond said to him: "That'll be twenty dollars and twenty-eight cents, Rockefeller...."

"What are you talking about?" said The Smooch.

"Ah, how easily we forget," said Raymond.

Then Raymond proceeded to give The Smooch a running total of what he owed him: "That'll be $12.48 for two cartons of Marlboro cigarettes."

"You're full of shit, Ray," The Smooch said to Raymond.

"And then there's $6.24 for the five Snickers bars I bought you Tuesday."

"What a cheapskate!"

"And then there's fifty-two cents for the two packs of bubble gum I bought you Tuesday along with the Snickers bars."

"Bull shit. I don't even chew bubble gum."

"Well, you did last week."

"Prove it, ass wipe!"

"And finally, your share of the beer and wine equals $4.14 divided by 4 equals one dollar and three-and-a-half cents which, rounded up to the nearest whole cent, equals $1.04 for a grand total of $20.28. Will that be by cash or by check, Sir?"

"Neither, douche bag," said The Smooch.

"Credit card, then?"

"No."

"Well, then I guess I'll just have to take it out in trade, won't I?"

"Go fuck yourself."

"I'd like my money, Smooch."

"You'll get your money, Ray. Relax, will you. What's the big rush all of a sudden?"

"When exactly?"

"When we get back to the apartment."

"Whose apartment?"

"My apartment."

"But we're not going back to your apartment. We're going back to *my* apartment."

"Well then, I'll pay you when we get to *your* apartment."

We started driving then to Ray's apartment.

***

Raymond's apartment building was conveniently located in an area of the East Village known as Alphabet City. Avenue B, I think—B for Booze. Either B for Booze or D for Drug Addicts. I forget which. One of them, though.

The apartment itself was quite a tiny affair: tiny living room, tiny bathroom, tiny bedroom—tiny everything. The only thing that wasn't tiny about it was Raymond's extremely extensive vinyl record collection. Oh, he had lots of records. Lots and lots of 'em. He had records in book shelves. He had records on top of book shelves. He had records in milk cartons. He had records in cardboard boxes.

Records records records and more records.

"Gee, Ray," I said to Raymond. "I had no idea that you were such a big record collector."

"Oh, sure, Frank. I'm a huge collector. I love music. All kinds of music."

"Well, why don't you play us one of your favorite records then?"

"Yeah, play us one of your favorite records, Ray." That was The Smooch obviously chiming in now—also a very big music lover.

"Well, what do you want to hear?" he said.

"Well, what have you got?" I said.

"Well, let's see now," Raymond said. "I've got The Goldberg Variations…."

"Excellent."

"I've got Sibelius's Violin Concerto…."

"Excellent."

"I've got his Fourth and his Seventh Symphonies…."

"Excellent."

"I've got Richter playing Schubert's *Wanderer Fantasy*…."

"Excellent."

"I've got—"

"—Have you got any Stones, Ray?"

"No, I don't have any Stones, Smooch."

"Well then how about Led Zeppelin?"

"No, I don't have any of that either."

"Well, then how about Finn Killian? I mean, you gotta have Finn Killian."

"Yeah, I've got some Finn Killian. You like Killian, Frank?"

"Yeah. Sure."

"Well, Killian it is then!"

Raymond put on the record.

After listening to Finn Killian for... oh, I don't know... maybe thirty seconds or so, I began to feel exactly the same way that I always did whenever I listened to Killian: Amused. Vaguely amused. In an extremely contemptuous or derisive manner. So this guy thought he could sing, huh? And millions of other people thought he could sing, too, huh? Jesus Christ, Finn. Give me a break, will you. Finn Killian was able to carry a tune the way that my Polish grandmother—who never went to school a day in her life and who milked goats back in The Old Country—was able to play Portia in *The Merchant Of Venice*. You know.... "The quality of mercy is not strained. It droppeth as the gentle rain from heaven" and so on. Yeah. That was Killian alright. Killian was Grandma. And not only was Killian Grandma—that would have been bad enough—that he was Grandma—but he *also*, as an added bonus, had this extremely peculiar... "other thing." This extremely peculiar affectation wherein, during the course of that abominable singing of his; or, rather, during the course of that abominable "non-singing" of his; or of that abominable "talk-singing" of his; or of that abominable "mock singing" of his; or of that abominable "anti-singing" of his; he would strategically *exaggerate* or *accentuate* certain critical, key, pivotal words. For instance, let's take one of his most popular tunes: *Dead Cat Bounce*. Now Killian—being Killian—isn't satisfied or content with merely "talk-singing" his refrain thusly:

How come you bounce
And you got all that pep
When you know that you're dead

'Cause you ain't got no head
And your nine lives have fled?

Oh no. Not F. K. That would have been too ordinary, too pedestrian for a sensibility as refined as his was. No. By the time Killian gets through giving the thing the full "Finn Killian Talk-Singing Treatment," it sounds a lot more like:

How come you BOWWWWWWWWWWWWWWWWWWNCE
And you got all that PEEEEEEEEEEEEEEEEEEEEEEEEEEEEEP
When you know that you're DEAAAAAAAAAAAAAAAAAAAAAAAAAD
'Cause you ain't got no HEAAAAAAAAAAAAAAAAAAAAAAAAAAAD
And your nine lives have—Etcetera etcetera etcetera etcetera.

I guess this is just Killian's charming way of really making it crystal clear to us that whatever person he is "talk-singing" about is really and truly as dead as a door nail—both spiritually as well as physically speaking, huh? That would certainly explain it, I'll wager. Or maybe—just *maybe*—Killian is going *beyond* merely STATING that the person in question is no longer with us. Maybe he's actually *gloating* about it! You know.... Happy about it. Positively *jubilant* about it. Which would also explain this endearing Killian affectation. So many theories.... So many viewpoints.... So many layers.... So many possible interpretations.... No wonder this guy has so many gold records to his credit. And—by the way—now that we're on the twin subjects of ineptitude and affectation, how about that killer rhyme scheme of his, huh?—*pep, dead, head, fled.* Wow. That really drives the old nail into the proverbial coffin too, don't you think? Genius. Sheer genius. That's what they all say, anyway—that he's a genius. A fucking genius. Well, maybe he really is a genius, just like maybe I'm really William Shakespeare. Or Albert Einstein. Or Donald Motherfucking Duck. Who knows? *Who knows?* Life is mysterious. It's very mysterious. And Art, too, is very mysterious. My turd is your masterpiece; and your masterpiece, my nightmare.

Anyway... at that point I said to the gang—just to give myself a little break from all of the "talk-singing" which was going on:

"Hey, Gang. Who wants some cigarettes?"

"I do!"

"I do!"

"My father—that sadistic scumbag—used to use my nubile body as his personal ashtray...."

"Okay then. That settles it. I'll be back in a few, guys. Party on!"

And then I removed myself from the lure of The Voice.

***

When I returned again, Ray was gone. So was The Mumbler—I mean Mary Poppins. Well, this is odd, I thought. This is very odd. Did Ray and Arielle hate Killian, too? I wondered.

"Hey, Smooch," I said.

"Yeah? What is it, Franklin?"

"Where'd they go, Smooch?"

"They're in the bedroom, moron."

"Well, what the heck are they doing in the bedroom?"

"Playing scrabble. You like scrabble, Frank?"

"Uh.... Sure, Smooch. I like scrabble."

"Yeah, me too. I *love* scrabble."

After it had been fully established that I liked scrabble and that The Smooch *loved* scrabble, I sat down again and continued drinking.

I continued drinking.

I continued smoking.

And I continued listening to Finn Killian.

"So tell me, Smooch," I finally said to The Smooch—cleverly initiating a conversation now with the dyed-in-the-wool Killian groupie in a last-ditch, heroic effort to try to "neutralize" the noxious effects which The Sirenian Crooner was, unfortunately, having upon me.... I said to him: "I don't mean to be nosy or anything, Smooch, but... just what exactly is it that you *do*, anyway? I mean... you never really talk about it."

"Well, that's because I don't like talking about it. I like keeping my personal shit personal, thank you."

"Yeah. Me too, Smooch. Gotcha."

"Oh, you got me, huh?"

"Absolutely. Lord knows, we already have enough Big Mouths running around all over the place."

"Big mouths, huh?"

"Yeah. You know…. Busy bodies. Vampires."

When I mentioned the word "vampires" to him, The Smooch perked up. He suddenly seemed to come to life.

"Hey, Franklin…."

"Yeah, Smooch?"

"Let me ask you a little question."

"Okay, Smooch. Ask away."

"Have you ever had sex with a woman before?"

"Excuse me?" I said to The Smooch.

"Excuse what?" The Smooch replied.

"I mean, what did you just say to me?"

The Smooch repeated the question.

"Well? Have you or haven't you?"

"Have you, Smooch?"

"Of course I have. You haven't, have you?"

"That's right."

"I knew it!" The Smooch said.

Knew it! Knew it! Knew it! Knew it!

Nailed it! Nailed it! Nailed it! Nailed it!

The Smooch did a little happy dance while he was busy congratulating himself on how well he'd nailed it.

"How did you know, Smooch?"

"Gee, I don't know, Frank. It just sort of came to me like… out of the blue."

"Well, then you must be some kind of a psychic or something."

"Yeah, that's me alright. I'm a psychic. I'm a goddamned fucking mind reader. You ever been arrested before?"

"What?"

"I said: have you have been arrested before?"

"Nope. Can't say that I have, Smooch. Never even got a parking ticket."

"How about prison then?"

"What do you mean how about prison then?"

"I mean have you ever spent any time in prison?"

"Well, if I've never been arrested before, then I've obviously never spent any time in prison."

"I was arrested, Franklin, and I've been in prison."

"*You* were arrested, Smooch? *You've* been in prison?"

"That's right, Frank."

"For how long?"

"Seven years."

"*Seven years!*"

"Yeah. Seven years."

"I don't believe it."

"Are you calling me a liar, Franklin?"

"No, Smooch. I'm not calling you a liar. I'm just... startled is all. You know.... Surprised."

"Well, what the hell are you so surprised about? What—you've never talked to an ex-con before?"

"As I matter, Smooch, no. I haven't."

"Well, you're looking at one now, kid. How does it feel, Frank?"

"It feels fine, Smooch."

"You don't feel dizzy or anything, do ya?"

"No, I don't feel dizzy or anything."

"No blurry vision?"

"No, no blurry vision."

"No chest pains?"

"No, no chest pains."

"Well, just give a holler, Frank, if you start having any chest pains. I tend to have that effect on civilians, you know. One guy, he peed in his pants when I told him. How's your bladder control?"

"It's excellent, Smooch."

"No leakage?"

"No. No leakage."

The Smooch continued on in this vein for a while, making like he was a medical doctor going through the usual obligatory review of systems.

Finally The Smooch said to me—not joking around now, but with perfect candor:

"You know, being locked up in prison is no joke, Frank. It changes a person."

"I'm sure it does, Smooch."

"It makes you hard."

"Yeah, but how did it happen, Smooch? I mean... how did it ever come to that?"

"What?"

"Going to prison obviously, you jerk. Being caged like a wild animal—and for seven years, no less! What are you—Al Capone or something?"

"No, Frank. I'm not Al Capone."

"Well, what then? Don't just leave me hanging, Smooch."

"You really want to know, huh?"

"Yeah. I do."

"Say please first."

"Alright. Please."

"Say pretty please—with cherries on top."

"Pretty please—with cherries on top."

"Okay. That's good. Now say—"

"Hey, fuck you, Smooch. Enough with the foreplay. Are you going to tell me or aren't you?"

"Alright, alright. Hold on to your horses, will ya. Jesus Christ. You're so impatient, Franklin...."

"I'm not impatient."

"No, you *are* impatient. You know, that's one of the first things I noticed right after I got out of the can."

"What?"

"How impatient all of you civilians are. What spoiled little brats you are. God forbid you should have to wait for a bus or something. Or for some waiter to bring you your fucking sushi. It's like life and death to you spoiled brats."

"I'm still waiting, Smooch. And I'm not getting any younger."

"Alright, alright. Sit down. Relax, will ya?"

I sat down and relaxed then. So did the Smooch. Then he proceeded to tell me the story.

He said to me: "Okay. Here it is. It's pretty simple and straightforward actually. Eight years ago—on The Fourth Of July—I'm barreling along on the old West Side Highway in my brand new Dodge Challenger—a birthday gift from Mommy and Daddy. I'm on my way to some new single's bar called *Movers And Shakers* around 70th & Broadway. It's around 10 or 10:30. A hot night. Really muggy. I get off at the Boat Basin and go zooming past Riverside. There's an old Chinese lady who's crossing the street. I didn't see anything. I just kept right on going. I was bombed out of my skull like you wouldn't believe, Franklin. The highway was floating. The Palisades looked so pretty. I thought the girls at the bar were all gonna fuck me."

"And you *killed* her?" I said.

"Well, I gave her a pretty good whack. At least that's what they told me, anyway. They told me her neck was broken, her spine was broken, her skull was busted, her spleen was gone."

"That's what they said to you—that her spleen was 'gone'?"

"Yeah."

"Gone, you mean, like in 'disappeared'?"

"Yeah."

"But how can that be, Smooch?"

"Gee, I don't know, Frank. I'm not a doctor. I just murder people when I'm as high as a kite."

"Jesus, Smooch."

"Yeah. Exactly, Franklin. You get the picture now?"

"Yeah. I get the picture."

We both paused then simultaneously immediately after I'd "gotten the picture."

Silence.

Total silence.

Presently, I said to my pal, the murderer:

"Well, how did you find out, Smooch? I mean, who told you? Who arrested you?"

"Two cops," The Smooch said. "Two assholes. Two nobodies. Mr. Good Cop and Mr. Bad Cop. Just like in the movies."

"I don't understand, Smooch."

"They tracked me down at the singles bar—Mr. Good Cop and Mr. Bad Cop. They must have been canvassing the entire neighborhood for eyewitnesses and shit. Makes sense, right?"

"Yeah. I guess."

"Mr. Bad Cop has a bull horn. A real bad ass motherfucker. He orders everybody in the singles bar to just 'SHUT THE FUCK UP!' and to 'TURN OFF THAT DAMNED MUSIC!' and to 'STOP SQUEALING LIKE LITTLE PUSSIES!' and so on, and so forth.... What a douche bag. Real Old School. Mr. Good Cop, on the other hand, is really sweet. He's Mr. Sensitive. He grabs the bull horn out of his partner's paws, and then he says to us diplomatically—like he's John Fucking Quincy Adams or something. Like he's Henry Fucking Cabot Lodge or something. He says to us: 'WE ARE EXTREMELY SORRY, LADIES AND GENTLEMAN, FOR THIS MOMENTARY INTERRUPTION. BUT DOES ANYBODY IN THIS SINGLES BAR HAPPEN TO OWN A YELLOW AND BLACK DODGE CHALLENGER?' I say to him: 'Yeah, Officer. I do. How come? Did I do something? Did I park it too close to a Tow Away Zone, Officer?' He says to me: 'Did you know that there's blood on the hood of your car, asshole?' Get that. Now he's calling me an 'asshole,' Franklin. No 'Mr.'

No 'Sir.' No '*Mr.* Asshole.' Just 'asshole.' Gee. I guess he wasn't so sensitive after all, huh? Anyway…. He asks me about the blood on the car, and I say to him: 'No, Officer. I didn't know that. Are you *sure* that it's blood, Officer? Are you sure that it's not… ketchup or something?' 'Ketchup?' he says to me. 'Yeah. Ketchup,' I say to him. 'You know…. The stuff you put on hot dogs and french fries? Hamburgers? Mozzarella sticks?' 'I know what ketchup is, asshole,' the guy says to me then, pissed. 'Yes. I'm sure that you do, Officer.' 'Well, then why the fuck did you just say that? What—do you think I'm retarded or something?' 'No, Officer. I don't. I don't think you're retarded or something. I'm just saying. That's all. I mean… they're both red, right? It's a common color.'

'HEY PHIL,' he says to his buddy, Phil, then. 'DO YOU HEAR THIS?'

'NO. WHAT, STEVE?'

'GUY SAYS THAT IT'S NOT BLOOD. SAYS HE WAS EATING A BIG MAC ON THE HOOD OF HIS CAR 'N SHIT.'

'NO KIDDING, STEVE!' Phil replies. 'A BIG MAC, HUH?'

'YEAH. WITH FRENCH FRIES. AND KETCHUP.'

Mr. Good Cop and Mr. Bad Cop both apologize then. Profusely. Mr. Good Cop—who is now Mr. Sensitive again—says to me—kind of wistfully: 'Well, you know what they say, Sir.' 'No. What do they say, Officer?' He says to me: 'To err is human, Sir; to forgive, divine.' And then they leave. Just like that."

"You're kidding me! *They left?*"

"Of course not. What's the hell's wrong with you?"

"Well, what really happened then?"

"Well, what do you think happened, stupid? They arrested me—obviously."

"You mean they cuffed you?"

"That's right."

"Read you your Miranda rights?"

"Exactly. Just like on *Kojak*."

"And then what?"

"And then—party time."

"What do you mean by that?"

"What?"

"Party time?"

"I mean we left. We drove off. I got to see the underbelly of our legal system really up close and personal. You know... party time. Howdy Doody time."

"Oh, right. Party time. I get it now."

"*You get it now?*"

"Well, not literally. I mean I don't 'get it now' the way that you 'got it.' I mean I *comprehend* it now. I mean I get the metaphor."

"Oh, you get *the metaphor*, do you?"

"Yeah. Exactly."

"Oh, well that's a load off, Frank."

"What is?"

"That you get THE METAPHOR. That you *grasp* THE METAPHOR. I mean... I was getting just a tad worried back there for a couple of seconds, amigo—thinking that you might not get THE METAPHOR. Because not everybody gets THE METAPHOR, you know. Only special people get THE METAPHOR."

"Okay, Smooch. You've made your point. You can stop laughing now."

He stopped laughing.

I said to The Smooch then—after he had stopped laughing, that is:

"So what happened next, Smooch? I mean... your parents must have gotten you a lawyer, right?—after they found out that you'd been arrested?"

"Uh-uh. Too expensive. My parents couldn't afford diddly."

"But you just said that they bought you a car, Smooch—a brand new Dodge Challenger. What does a Challenger cost these days, Smooch? Five grand? Six grand?"

"Nah. Seven's more like it."

"Seven grand, huh?"

"Yeah. At least."

"So… what was the big deal then? What was the hold up? Why no lawyer?"

"The 'hold up,' Frank, was that my parents were destitute."

"Destitute?"

"Yeah. As in 'penniless.' You see, everything they ever bought in life was always paid for using a line of credit."

"Everything, Smooch?"

"EVERYTHING. Credit cards…. Home equity…. A third mortgage…. Deferred leasing…. You name it—they borrowed it. They were like… role models for the American Middle Class."

"But I still don't understand, Smooch. I mean… if borrowing was the only way that your parents could ever afford to buy anything, then why didn't they just take out another loan for a good trial lawyer?"

"Oh, they tried, Frank. Believe me. First thing they did was run to the bank and try to get another home equity loan. The loan officer laughed in their faces. Called 'em Bozo and Clarabell—same as the shylocks."

"Well, did The State at least provide you with legal counsel? You know… after they arrested you and before the arraignment?"

"Oh, so you know all about arraignments too, huh?"

"Well… just what I've learned from watching *Kojak*, Smooch."

The Smooch chuckled then—but it was a hollow chuckle. "Very funny," he said. "Good one, asshole."

"Sorry, Smooch," I said. "Mea culpa."

"Mea what?" he said.

"Never mind," I said.

Then he said to me, in all seriousness:

"Yeah, Frank. There was an arraignment alright. And—yes—I did indeed get 'legal counsel.' Some yuppie prick fresh out of Law School. He was about as interested in my case as I was in his shit fantasies about becoming Attorney General. Not exactly Clarence Darrow, Franklin."

"So… what happened next, Smooch?"

"What happened next? I pleaded guilty to one count of vehicular homicide while driving under the influence of alcohol, hashish, Valium, and oxycontin. Seeing as how this was my second D.W.I. in less than nine months, the judge threw the book at me."

"What does that mean—he threw the book at you?"

"It means that he gave me the maximum sentence allowable by law."

"Which was?"

"Seven to twelve years in a maximum security penitentiary, eligible for parole after the first seven. I spent another three days in a cell at Rikers before they carted my ass off to prison."

"What prison did they ship you off to?"

"Ossining."

"You mean Sing Sing?"

That's right, Frank. Good old Sing Sing. Last know postal address of such inspirational role models as Louis Lepke, Albert Fish, Gary Evans, Ruth Snyder, Martha Place, David Berkowitz and, of course, let's not forget our favorite two commie traitors, Mr. & Mrs. Julius and Ethel Rosenberg, may their framed souls rest in peace."

"Holy shit, Smooch! This is killing me! *You mean to tell me that you actually went to the same prison where they locked up Son Of Sam?*"

"That's right, Frank. Pretty cool, huh?"

"Well…. I wouldn't exactly call it 'cool,' Smooch."

"Oh, no?"

"No."

"Well, what would you call it then?"

"How about shocking? How about appalling? How about horrific? How about surreal?"

"Surreal, huh?"

"Yeah. *Beyond* terrifying. I mean… *so far* beyond 'terrifying' so that you don't even think it's happening to you—even though you *know* it's happening to you."

"Well, you got that one right, pal. It was definitely pretty fucking 'surreal.' Took me a good two to three solid months to finally come out of 'The Surreal Phase' and then to slowly wean myself into the next one."

"And what was the next one?"

"The Diarrhea Phase."

"Excuse me?"

"I said The Diarrhea Phase. The Runs Phase. Have you ever had a bad case of the runs, Frank?"

"Yeah. Sure."

"Well, multiply it by seven years then. Seven years times 365 equals what, Frank?"

"I dunno, Smooch."

"Well, I do. It equals 2,555 days of diarrhea. That's a lot of toilet paper, don't you think, amigo?"

"Gee, I dunno, Smooch."

"Trust me, Franklin. It's *a lot!* Every time I take a shit now and wipe my asshole, I think about it."

"Think about what, Smooch?"

"About the toilet paper. About that lovely lovely lovely toilet paper. Two ply. One ply. *Any* ply. It's all good."

There was a temporary lull in the conversation at that point—not that the conversation was over by any means. There was still lots of stuff left to talk about. This was just the appetizer—not the entrée. But just like anybody who's a natural writer—a natural writer—a natural painter—a natural musician—an artistic person—The Smooch paced himself as he told his story. He didn't rush it. He took his time about it, telling his tale at a leisurely enough pace so that I was able to follow it without any difficulty, but not so leisurely so as to bore me to death. He struck just the right balance. The art of story-telling, I am convinced, is basically the same art as The Art Of Seduction: knowing when to hold back and when to come on strong. Knowing how to set a trap and when to "spring it." Not many are able to do this—not even your so-called "Seduction Authorities" and "Seduction Police." Oh, they can certainly talk a good game alright—all of these so-called "Seduction Authorities" and "Seduction Police"—only when it comes right down to it—they don't have it. *They don't have it!* But The Smooch did. The Smooch definitely "had it."

Lucky for him that he didn't know he "had it"—because if he *had* known, that would have probably killed it.

Fucking Smooch. That fucking yahoo....

Anyway.... After The Smooch—that fucking yahoo—had held back long enough in that particular stage of The Grand Seduction, he said to me, rather innocuously:

"Hey, Franklin."

"Yeah, Smooch?"

"Can I ask you another question?"

"Yeah, sure Smooch. Go ahead."

"Have you ever been fucked in the ass before, Franklin?"

"Excuse me? Come again?"

"I said: Have you ever been fucked in the ass before?"

"Jesus Christ, Smooch! What a question!"

"Well? Have you or haven't you?"

"No, Smooch. I haven't."

"I have!" The Smooch boasted.

"You have, Smooch?"

"Oh absolutely. That's the one stereotype about prison life that's a thousand percent on the level, Franklin. Either you let 'em corn hole you or you get decapitated—or both maybe—if you even *look* at them funny. And there isn't a damned thing that you can do about it."

"Nothing, Smooch?"

"No. Nothing, Franklin."

"Well, how often does it happen exactly?"

"Well, how often do you take a shower, Franklin?"

"I don't take showers, Smooch. I take baths."

"Well, that would obviously change rapidly once they dropped you off at your new digs."

"You have a boyfriend while you were in prison, Smooch?"

"Did I have a *what* while I was in prison, Franklin?"

"You know. A boyfriend. A steady sodomizer."

"Oh, that's rich, Frank! That's really rich! Yeah. Like we all had boyfriends and girlfriends and high school crushes and Senior proms."

"You know what I mean, Smooch."

"Yeah, I know what you mean, Franklin."

"Well? Did you?"

"Yeah. Kind of."

"What was his name, Smooch?"

"Norman The Doorman."

"What?"

"We used to call him Norman The Doorman."

"Well, what did you call him that for?"

"Because a) Norman The Doorman's first name was Norman, and because b) Norman The Doorman had actually once been a doorman. Said he used to work at The Plaza, and then at The Waldorf Astoria."

"And then what?"

"Big career move. Norman The Doorman suddenly became Norman The Axe Murderer. Norman The Rapist. Norman The Gang Banger. Norman The Boyfriend."

"Oh."

"Then I had another 'boyfriend' after Norman died."

"Oh, yeah?"

"Yeah."

"And what was his name?"

"Adolph The Meat Tenderizer. You want to know why we called him Adolph The Meat Tenderizer, Frank?"

"Let me take a wild guess, Smooch: Because a) his name was Adolph, and because b) he was a meat tenderizer?"

"Exactly, Franklin. He was an expert meat tenderizer."

"Say, didn't any of you wacko miscreants have ordinary, normal nicknames?"

"Well, what do you mean by 'normal nicknames'?"

"You know. Normal nicknames. Common nicknames. Like, say, 'Spike' or 'Butch' or 'Tiny' or 'Red'?"

"Well, let me see now...." The Smooch began thinking about it. "Hm.... Well, we had Norman, of course. And then we had Adolph, of course. And then we had The Snake Pit. And The Swamp Thing. And The Tooth Fairy. And Hairy Lester. And then there was Jimmy Boot Straps. And Jimmy Soul Train. And Jimmy Coke Bottles. We had a lot of Jimmy's."

"But no Tiny's, huh?"

"No. No Tiny's, Frank. All of the nicknames were like... really quirky."

Suddenly The Smooch thought of something. Something exciting, it seemed. Something which, maybe, I just might find kind of interesting.

"Well, you know, there was this one guy who used to work in the laundry room...."

"What one guy?"

"You know. With a 'normal' nickname."

"What was the nickname?"

"We used to call him 'Scar Face'."

"Well, praise the Lord and pass the ammunition!" I said. "Finally," I said. "A *normal* nickname!"

"Well, not really, Franklin."

"No?"

"No. Turns out that Scar Face's boyfriend caught him giving a blow job to this other dude—"

"What other dude?"

"Some Nazi skin head."

"Oh."

"Anyway, the first guy—I mean the boyfriend—wasn't exactly what you'd call 'the forgiving type'."

"Why? What did he do, Smooch? Cut his balls off?"

"Not exactly, Franklin. But something almost as bad."

"What?"

"He takes a *pencil*—you know? A plain old garden variety #2 lead pencil that you'd buy at The Dollar Store, or at Woolworths, or at the supermarket, or at a fucking newsstand—and then he carves his face up pretty good with it when 'the unfaithful bitch' is giving *him* a blow job."

"Oh, gross!"

"Yeah. Exactly. You know, a pencil, Franklin—*a simple pencil*—can do an awful lot of fucking damage in the proper hands—and with the proper attitude."

"And just what exactly is 'the proper attitude'?"

"Wanting to make a big splash. Wanting to be as bloody as possible. I mean... if being as bloody as possible is what floats your boat, Franklin, then a little good old fashioned 'pencil surgery' should definitely fill the bill. But then... there are also *other ways* that aren't bloody. Lots of neat ways. Lots of clean ways. Did you know, for instance, that you can kill a guy just by rolling a magazine up into the shape of a cone and then stabbing him in the chest with it? That's called 'the jammerz.' It won't penetrate the epidermis of course—the way that a knife will or a box cutter—but the sheer, concentrated force alone should be more than sufficient to get the job done. As a matter of fact, Franklin m' boy, now that we're on the subject of extremely low-tech but efficient prison weaponry, I would have to say in all honesty that the jammerz definitely takes the cake. No muss, no fuss. Just the simple beauty of blunt force trauma. One time I saw this guy get it with an ice pick as well as the jammerz. Now *that*, my friend, was really interesting. The ice pick worked like a charm, of course. Made a fucking mess like you wouldn't believe. *And yet, Franklin.... And yet!*"

"And yet what, Smooch?"

"It was *The Popular Mechanics* that actually killed the dude—not the ice pick. I mean... what's an ice pick compared to the jammerz, right?"

"Gee, I don't know, Smooch. What *is* an ice pick compared to the jammerz?"

"Look. An ice pick is like a .22, okay? Can it kill you, Frank? Yeah. Sure it can kill you. But the jammerz is like... a .45. It's like a shotgun. Filled with double-aught buck shot! Doesn't matter where you get it. You're gonna die, my friend, no matter where you get it."

The Smooch shook his head then, and he smiled wistfully—with great tenderness—as if he were lamenting something. His lost youth, probably. "Prison," he was thinking (probably), "where art thou? Where goest thou? Wherefore, Cruel Mistress, dost thou abandon me now in my sorest hour? You were a salacious trollop—to be sure—but at least, Dearest, you were *my* trollop: Three square meals a day and a firm mattress without any bed bugs. Every day. Every week. Every month. Every year. What more could a cuckold ask for? You were perfection, Dearest. You were the cat's meow...."

That sort of a wistful smile. It was really heartbreaking to see him suffer so.

"You know, Smooch.... I was just wondering about something," I said to The Smooch then—very gently—immediately after he had returned safe and sound from his nostalgic trip down Memory Lane.

"Oh, yeah?"

"Yeah."

"And what's that?"

"Well, in all of the time that I've been coming to The Shit Hole and drinking beer with you degenerate assholes, I've never actually seen you talk to even one single, solitary female—let alone try scoring with any of them. You still attracted to women, Smooch?"

"What a question, Franklin! What a stupid question!"

"Well? Are you or aren't you?"

"Of course I'm still attracted to women, you jerk. Being butt fucked while you're doing time doesn't instantaneously make you a faggot, you know—or didn't they teach you that in that fancy college of yours?"

I didn't answer the question, it being a rhetorical question. Or at least I *assumed* that it was a rhetorical question. Knowing the difference between a rhetorical question and a *real* question was one of my few strong points—although I had learned it way before going to college.

"Of course… if I was rotting away in some stinking hell hole for like… thirty-five or forty years or something, well then—yeah—maybe *then* I'd just wanna get butt fucked. But seven years ain't that long a stretch, Frank—not enough to make me a homo, anyway."

"Well, good for you, Smooch! What an accomplishment!"

"Yeah, I guess it is an accomplishment, isn't it?"

"Well, I should think so."

"Yeah. Me, too. I guess that makes me John Motherfucking Wayne, huh?"

"Sure."

"Gary Motherfucking Cooper?"

"Check."

"Audie Motherfucking Murphy?"

"Why not?"

"You know, Audie Murphy killed a lot of krauts, Frank. I think he killed like… the most krauts of any guy fighting in World War II."

"Well, that's what they say, Smooch."

"What a hero. I betcha Audie Murphy never took it up the ass, Franklin."

"Probably not, Smooch."

"Guaranteed. Audie Murphy would've probably turned some homo kraut into link sausages. You know what I mean, Frank?"

"Yeah. Definitely. So tell me, Smooch…."

"Tell you what, Frank?"

"What other kinds of disgusting things happened to you while you were in the joint, Smooch—other than getting raped, that is?"

"Oh, lots of stuff. Lots of nasty shit."

"Like what, for instance?"

"Like getting my feelings hurt. I mean, if you don't like getting your feelings hurt—if you're the shy, retiring, sensitive type—then stay out of the joint, Franklin."

"Yeah, I'll definitely keep that in mind, Smooch."

"Yeah. Do that. Seriously do that. And stay away from drugs too, kid! Drugs are bad news. Drugs will kill ya. You'll never become a plastic surgeon by taking drugs, chief. Mark my words."

"Who said anything about becoming a plastic surgeon?"

"I mean a professional person. A guy with money. You know.... A doctor. A lawyer. A banker. An Indian chief."

"Oh."

"Well, maybe you can become a banker. I mean... bankers rule, right?"

"Yeah. Right."

"But not a doctor. And not a lawyer. And definitely not an Indian chief."

"Okay, Smooch. Point noted. But can we get back now to the original question?"

"What original question?"

"About what life was like while you were incarcerated."

"Well, what exactly do you want to know about it?"

"I want to know what else happened there."

"Oh, lots of stuff. Lots of bad stuff."

"You already said that."

"Yeah. And I meant it, too!"

"Aw, come on, Smooch. Give me some details, will ya?"

"Oh, so you want details, do you?"

"Yes. Please."

The Smooch paused then—for yet a second time—in the implementation of The Grand Seduction. He was probably thinking to himself at this point: To disclose or not to disclose.... To shock or not to shock.... To repulse or not to repulse.... To edit out or to leave in.... So many questions.... So many choices.... The art of seduction involves lots of decision-making. Finally, after he had made his decisions— selected just the right path, the right approach, the right tone, the right everything—he said to me, rather provocatively:

"Well, I'll tell you, Franklin.... "

"Yes. Do, Smooch."

"Since you seem to have taken such a keen interest in the wild, wooly world of Penology—"

"Oh, I have Smooch. I definitely have. After all, Smooch, you're my first murderer."

"Aw, shucks, Frank. It ain't nothin'."

"No. It's something, Smooch. It's definitively something."

The Smooch really seemed to "light up" when I said that to him—about its being something.

Then he said to me:

"Okay then. Fine. But let me ask you a little question first."

"Yeah. Sure, Smooch. Ask away."

"Have you ever seen any of those old prison movies—you know, the old Classics from the thirties and forties like: *Each Dawn I Die, The Big House, Men Without Souls, San Quentin, Brute Force, I Am a Fugitive On a Chain Gang*, and so on?"

"Yeah, sure, Smooch. I mean—some of them."

"Well, all that stuff's bunk. It's all horse shit. It's just some lame Hollywood Jew fantasy concocted by sheltered Mama's boys who knew nothing about it. I mean… *maybe* life in the joint was really like that back in the day before computers 'n shit. But those days are long gone, pal. Nowadays, when they send you to prison for Vehicular Homicide or Manslaughter Two, you gotta get yourself hooked up to a gang. A really well-established gang. With clout. They send you away and you're not part of a gang, Frank—that's like being Jesse Jackson at a Clan rally. You leave yourself wide open."

"Well…. Just how many kinds of gangs are we talking about here, Smooch?"

"Shit. I don't know, Franklin. Twenty…. Thirty…. Thirty-five…. Sixty, maybe…. It all depends on where they send you. If they send you to a facility on the West Coast, for example—like Obispo—in California—there's like… 92 different kinds of Mexican gangs. Then you got your classic white supremacist gangs, biker gangs, black Muslim gangs, Puerto Rican gangs, Cuban gangs, Tex Mex gangs, Whop gangs, Roosky gangs, Bible Belt Hell Fire 'N Damnation gangs, Jew gangs, Albanian gangs, Serbian gangs, Macedonian gangs...."

"Well, what kind of gang did you belong to, Smooch?"

"Me? I was part of something called the Unitarian Zionist Aryan Brotherhood—UZABs for short."

"Wow. Sounds really impressive, Smooch."

"Oh, it was impressive alright. And exclusive, too! First you had to take an IQ test. Nobody who got an IQ over 100 was allowed in. And then you had to get a recommendation from either a serial rapist or an axe murderer— preferably from an axe murderer. You think *Harvard* is tough getting into? Well, then try getting into the UZABs, chief. That'll rock your world. Screw Harvard."

"Leave it to you, Smooch, to join a Hitler gang—I mean, that's what it was, right?"

"Yeah. Right. They hated kikes, of course. They hated niggers, of course. Mexicans.... Puerto Ricans.... Cubans.... Armenians.... Turks.... Arabs.... Rooskies.... Polaks.... Micks.... Rumanians.... Yugoslavians—you name it! Basically anybody who wasn't a Nazi."

"You ever have to kill anybody for the UZABs, Smooch?"

"Nah." The Smooch dismissed the question with a wave of his hand. "Me and violence are kind of like oil and water. Just isn't my thing. I'm really a hippie at heart. All I had to do to keep my head on my shoulders was play A) 'Mrs. Norman The Doorman' and then B) 'Mrs. Adolph The Meat Tenderizer.' It was a pretty good life, Frank. I mean, I'm not complaining or anything. There was always plenty of food on the table just as long as you kept your men happy."

"Well, about that...."

"About what, Frank?"

"This whole 'food on the table' business."

"Yeah, Frank? What about it?"

"That brings me to my next question."

"What question?"

"About drugs."

"Well, what about 'em?"

"Were drugs rampant?"

"What—in prison?"

"No, Smooch. At the public library."

"What a question! What a stupid question! That's like asking me whether water is wet."

"So I take it, then, that drugs were rampant."

"Oh, they were more than just rampant, baby. Drugs were IT. You wanted to buy something—a copy of *Playboy*—a jar of Vaseline—a new pencil case—with a pencil sharpener—you paid with heroin. You paid with coke. You paid with pot. You paid with quaaludes. The wheels of prison, my friend, are greased with quaaludes."

"So… you're saying that quaaludes were the most popular drugs then?"

"No, not popular, Frank. *Prevalent.* Heroin was the most popular drug. Only… heroin is very expensive, Frank. And they always cut it down to almost nothing! So you had to settle for quaaludes and decent pot. Valium…. Stool softeners…. Sometimes the Mexicans would give the UZAB's oregano instead of real pot, or baking soda instead of heroin, and then there would be WAR. I mean really blood-curdling, nasty shit. Sometimes fifteen—maybe twenty—guys would get the jammerz in less than thirty seconds. It would be over that quickly—and then everything would be back to normal again."

"Whatever 'normal' was."

"Yeah. Exactly. I personally witnessed one guy get his little pinky finger chopped off by a four-foot-long bolt cutter just to teach him a lesson when he sold 'em talcum powder. They're kind of touchy about that sort of thing. Particularly the Colombians. They hate talcum powder. You give 'em talcum powder instead of coke and you're going to walk away from the experience minus an appendage, my friend. Guaranteed."

"Wow. That's absolutely amazing, Smooch. So brutal…. So

frightening…. I mean the way you describe it, it's like being back in The Stone Age."

"Yeah, that would be one way of putting it—mildly. Being back in The Stone Age. Living with dinosaurs."

"But what about the guards, Smooch?"

"Well, what about the guards, Franklin?"

"I mean, surely the guards didn't just twiddle their thumbs while all of this mayhem was going down, right?"

"Hey, let me tell you a little something about civil servants in penitentiaries, College Boy. These morally bankrupt, sadistic scumbags were far worse than any of the 'dinosaurs' were. Hey, I'll take a 'dinosaur' any day over one of these morally bankrupt, sadistic scumbags."

"But… were they really as terrible as all that, Smooch? I mean… *all* of them? Every one of them?"

"That's right, Franklin. *Every one of them!*"

"Incredible, Smooch."

"As God is my witness. Hey, do you wanna know what these morally bankrupt, sadistic scumbags used to do to us inmates just for kicks?"

"What, Smooch? What'd they do to you?"

"Well, every Tuesday evening at 7 sharp—just like clockwork—we'd have 'Movie Night.'"

"What do you mean you'd have 'Movie Night?'"

"I mean every Tuesday at 7 sharp—without fail—they'd wheel out this old, beat up, World War II movie projector and play movies 'n shit in the cafeteria."

"So what's so terrible about that, Smooch? I mean… I would think that showing you movies would be a *good* thing—not a bad thing. You know…. Something to look forward to. To break up the monotony."

"No, no. You don't understand, Franklin. These psycho pricks were making fools of us. They'd play the most trivial, ridiculous, empty-headed, feathery bull shit. Mind-numbing, meaningless junk that turns your brain into silly putty. Makes you drool. Shit yourself. You know what I'm talking about, right Frank?"

"No, Smooch. What are you talking about?"

"I'm talking about *Father Of The Bride*. I'm talking about *Meet Me In St. Louis*. I'm talking about *The Wizard Of Oz*. I'm talking about *White Christmas*. I'm talking about *Miracle On 34th Street*. I'm talking about *It's A Wonderful Life*. I'm talking about *Gold Diggers Of 1933*, *Gold Diggers Of 1935*, *Gold Diggers Of 1937*, and just about every motherfucking movie ever made starring Fred Astaire and Ginger Rogers. Jesus, Franklin…. It was like torture. It was like having fucking root canal without any novocaine."

"Jesus, Smooch. I had no idea…."

"Well, how could you, Frank? How could anybody? Nobody but an ex-con would have even the foggiest idea of what I'm talking about."

"Evidently," I said to The Smooch.

"And here's another little tid bit for you that you civilian sushi eaters would never know about."

"What?"

"Out of all of those toxic movies that those sadistic cocksuckers would force feed us, it turns out that *Gold Diggers Of 1933* was actually the most toxic."

"What do you mean, Smooch?"

"I mean this, Franklin: Every time one of those sadistic cocksuckers would drag out that monstrosity and play it for us at top volume, somebody would invariably kill himself. You'd either swallow rat poison when you were back in your cage again; hang yourself with one of your shoe laces; smack your head against the wall and crack your skull open; stick your head in the toilet bowl and drown yourself; slit your wrists with a box cutter; roll up a copy of *Penthouse* or *Playboy* and then do a little 'jammerz' number on yourself…. Shit like that, Frank. It never failed."

"Jesus, Smooch. That's really something."

"Oh, it was something alright. To know it was to love it. And to love it was to lose it. Even to this very day, Franklin, I still get sick to my stomach anytime anybody *even mentions* Dick Powell or Ruby Keeler to me."

"No kidding?"

"No kidding."

"Well, I won't mention 'em then."

"Yeah. I would really appreciate it."

At that point The Smooch shuttered. He shuttered violently. Like he was suddenly freezing to death.

***

The next day after math class, I immediately ran up to Raymond and confronted him head on, saying to him:

"Holy shit, Raymond! What the fuck!"

"What?"

"What's up with your little side kick?"

"What little side kick?"

"You know…. Mr. 'I-Went-To-Sing-Sing-For-Killing-An-Old-Chinese-Lady-And-Shared-Dorm-Space-With-David-Berkowitz.' That little side kick. Why the hell didn't you tell me, Ray?"

Raymond laughed then. Raymond belly laughed—like the way you'd belly laugh while you were reading *Post Office*, for example. Like the way you'd belly laugh when Bukowski writes around all of the mangy dogs which used to terrorize him while he was trying to deliver the mail on his daily routes—particularly one fully grown German shepherd. Oh, that was funny! That was really funny. That was kind of the way Raymond belly laughed when I broached the subject of "The Incarceration."

"What's so funny, dick weed?" I said to Raymond. "You want to let me in on the big joke?"

"Yeah. Sure, Frank. No problem. But brace yourself first, amigo, because it's gonna be a rough landing."

114

"Alright, Ray. I'm braced. I've got my head crouched between my knees and I've got my hands laced over the top of it. Now go ahead, asshole. Give it to me."

Ray gave it to me then—straight—very simply and very directly, saying:

"Sorry to have to burst your bubble, Franklin, but The Smooch ain't no ex-con. He's just a lowly, insignificant grad student doing his dissertation on Dostoyevsky. The closest that Murray—A/K/A "The Smooch"—Grelsmar ever came to being in what you'd call 'lockdown' was reading *Crime And Punishment* in his parents' finished basement."

I shook my head then exceedingly slowly while taking a gander at my Adidas sneakers. My Adidas sneakers looked completely shot—like I'd been working for the last twenty years as a grease monkey or a coal miner. Presently I said to Raymond:

"But I don't understand, Ray. Why the hell would he say all that? Why go through all of the trouble of creating some... elaborate fantasy?"

"That's just the way he is, Frank. The guy is an asshole. A real wise-ass. God knows why he does it. Maybe it's just his Big Way of getting back at his Mommy for not having sufficiently breastfed him."

"So his mother didn't sufficiently breastfeed him?"

"No—no. That's just an example, Frank. I have absolutely no idea how much he was breastfed—or even if he was breastfed."

"Oh."

"All I'm saying is that he seems to have some kind of an axe to grind."

"What kind of an 'axe'?"

"Beats me. You'd have to ask Murray about his 'axe' collection."

"Yeah. Right, Ray. Like he'd really tell me."

"Funny thing is—in 'real life'—he's really a very shy, retiring person. Quiet. Very quiet. Very reserved around the opposite sex. I know he likes 'em but he's practically celibate. My sister and all of her girlfriends think he's some kind of nerdy loser or something. You know. Some Alfred E. Newman type who's trying really hard to pretend he isn't. Granted, he's an acquired taste. I mean, he's not for everyone. But I really dig him."

"Jesus, Ray. I'm such as asshole."

"You're not an asshole. You just don't know Murray is all. Believe me, it's not just you, Franklin. The guy is a dick weed around practically everybody— especially other grad students. He's a practical joker with the soul of a seven year old."

I looked down again at my filthy sneakers. I shook my head again. I closed my eyes. After I had reopened them, I said to Raymond:

"And to think that I actually shared thoughts with this creep. Talked about Jean Genet with him. Talked about *Our Lady Of The Flowers* with him…."

"Our lady of the what?"

"Never mind. Doesn't matter now."

Suddenly Raymond thought of something. Something funny. Something extremely funny. The new thought which suddenly occurred to him was like an added bonus to an already perfect present—the maraschino cherry on top of the hot fudge sundae.

"Did he tell you the part about Norman The Doorman?"

"Yeah."

"How about the UZABs?"

"That, too."

"How about *Gold Diggers Of 1933*? Did he tell you about that, too, Franklin?"

I shook my head again—very slowly.

"Oh, this is beautiful, Franklin! Just *bee-you-tee-full!* You know, The Smooch doesn't discuss the UZABs and that Busby Berkeley shit with just anybody. Murray must really like you, Frank. I mean… you must have really impressed the guy something awful for him to have spilled the beans about *The Gold Diggers*."

"Well, bully for me," I said. "That, and four bits," I said.

"You know, me and Murray go way back, Frank. We went to the same Middle School in Larchmont together…. Played soccer together…. Smoked dope together…. His mother and my mother even used to drive down to Bally's together. Son of a bitch used to have acne and wear braces. Such a shy, ugly, reclusive nerd!"

"Well, he's not shy anymore, Ray. He's got a real mouth on him, that one."

"You angry, Frank?"

"Well… sort of. I mean… yeah. I mean, wouldn't you be?"

"Yeah. I suppose so."

"You *suppose* so?"

"Well, you have to understand, Frank. I don't get angry anymore. I'm beyond anger."

"You're *beyond* anger?"

"Well, not *entirely* beyond it. But I'm making terrific strides. I mean, I'm *almost* beyond it. I'm like… *semi*-beyond it."

"Sounds nice, Ray—to be beyond anger."

"Oh, it is nice. It's very nice. Only problem is, it takes a lot out of you."

"What?"

"Going beyond it. Re-directing it. And, unfortunately, I'm not always up to the task."

"Me neither, Ray. I'm almost never up to it. Which is precisely why I'm so angry at Murray."

"Oh, about that…."

"Yeah, what about it?"

"Well, I'll tell you what I gonna do, Frank—seeing as how you're now an official UZAB."

"An official UZAB or just an honorary UZAB?"

"No. An official UZAB. A *certifiable* UZAB. I mean… I think you've earned it. Don't you?

"How so, Ray?"

"Very simple. Just by being taken in by all of that insufferable, inane drivel of his. I mean… just how long did he actually go on about it?"

"Gee, I don't know, Ray. Half an hour, maybe…."

"You're kidding me, Frank! *Half an hour?*"

"Yeah."

"Half an hour of having to listen to some adolescent, lame fantasy about sodomy behind bars, huh?"

"Yeah, I guess so."

"You guess so?

"Well, it could have been a little longer."

"How long, Frank?"

"Forty minutes, maybe. I mean, when he started lighting into the prison guards and waxing eloquent about 'Movie Night'—that alone was pretty detailed. Jesus, Raymond. The guy could shovel it."

"Well, there you go then! That settles it. Welcome to the club, Brother."

"Gee thanks, Ray—I mean, Fellow UZAB."

Raymond saluted me at that point. I saluted him back. I guess that made it official.

"Anyway…. Like I was just saying, Franklin…."

"Yes, Brother? What were you just saying?"

"Seeing as how you're now a member of one of the most exclusive prison gangs in the entire country—"

"—Oh, I can't believe it, Ray! Me—a UZAB! An *actual* UZAB! I never thought I'd live to see the day!"

Raymond paused respectfully at that point while I came to grips with it—I mean, with the *hugeness* of it. The unparalleled grandiosity of it. Why, it was almost like being told that you were going to die of some incurable disease in six weeks; *and then* being told that you were not going to die in six weeks—that it was just some stupid clerical lab error. That kind of unparalleled grandiosity. Presently my Pre-Calculus math teacher said to me in The Great Spirit Of UZAB Brotherhood:

"Hey, here's an idea! What do you say, my Highly Esteemed, Highly Honorable, Unitarian Zionist Aryan Brother-In-Arms, that I give you an A plus instead of a D minus in this retarded math class that I'm stuck having to teach you? How does that grab you, Brother? Do you think you can handle it?"

"My God, Ray. Do you really mean it?"

"Of course I mean it. Why wouldn't I mean it?"

"Gee, I don't know, Ray. I'm just a little confused is all. I mean, first you tell me that I'm an official UZAB—which is like this… totally gratuitous 'dream-come-true' for me; and now you're telling me that I'm an A plus math student! It's all happening so quickly, Ray. It's like a tidal wave. It's overwhelming!"

"Get a grip on yourself, will you, Brother. We UZABs have to stick together, right?"

"Right."

"I mean… it's us against them, isn't it?"

"Who's 'them,' Ray?"

"Them is everybody. You know…. Everybody who isn't US: The blacks, the Jews, The Armenians, the Rooskies, The Irish, The Italians…. Didn't The Smooch explain it to you?"

"He certainly did, Ray. In exquisite detail."

"Well, there you go, then! Enjoy the ride, Genius! Glad to have you aboard the UZAB train."

"Raymond, you're beautiful."

"I'm not beautiful."

"No, you *are* beautiful. And Mommy's gonna think you're beautiful, too. In fact, Mommy's gonna think you're *so* beautiful that she's gonna want to cook you a whole mess of delicious dinners right after she sees that stellar grade that you're gonna be giving me."

"Oh, I'm glad, Frank! I'm so glad! I'd just love to meet Mrs. Cohen. Say, how's Mrs. Cohen's meatloaf, by the way?"

"Oh, she makes a really, really awesome meatloaf. Not too mushy. Lots of gravy. You wouldn't think that such a sick woman could make such an unbelievably delicious meatloaf, would ja? But she can, Ray. She really can! She's like this… mad-as-a-hatter Julia Child or something."

"Well, meatloaf it is then! Shall we say… Sunday evening? Around seven-ish? I'll bring the Merlot. Or would you prefer Chardonnay?"

"Raymond, you're beautiful."

"You already said that."

"Well, I'm saying it again then. You know, not everybody gets my jokes, Ray. In fact, most humans don't even have any."

"Have any what, Frank?"

"A sense of humor. A bone dry, ironic wit. What planet did you say you're from again?"

"I didn't say."

"No, of course you didn't."

Our eyes locked for a just second then. But it was a miraculous second. It spoke volumes.

4. IN THE DOLDRUMS – AGAIN

I washed out of NYU shortly after the spring break. After the spring break, I had had quite enough of it. Enough of the Biology. Enough of the Physics. Enough of the Chemistry—especially the Chemistry. The Organic Chemistry and the Introductory Biology broke the proverbial camel's back, so to speak. Fuck this, I said to myself. Fuck Ragnar. Fuck Beverly. Fuck Beverly's parents. Fuck my parents. My parents and Beverly's parents were the reason why shrinks made so much obscene money. Why they had summer houses in Provence, and had the leisure time to write so many silly papers. The world is a madhouse and most people are lost within it. A shrink can't change that. Pills can't change that. Pills can numb you to the madness to a certain extent. Only… who in their right mind wants to go through life being numb to everything— including beauty? Not me. That's for damned sure. I'd rather face the madness head on and go out swinging, like a winner….

For a short while, I did nothing. I mean… I read a lot—but then I always read a lot. If I was in the toilet, shitting—I would read on the toilet seat. If I was at the doctor's office, waiting, I would read in the waiting room. If I was throwing up or if I had a fever—well… then I wouldn't read. That was different. But otherwise, I was always reading something. Some novel or other. Some story or other. Some essay or some poem. Anything. By any author. Just as long as it was a meticulous author who gave you nothing less than his total meticulousness.

Good writer—good reader.

Great writer—great reader.

Careless writer—careless reader.

Shitty writer—postmodern art critic.

I also continued to drive into Manhattan—down to The Shit Hole—which had become almost like a second home to me. Raymond—my fellow alien from a far away, distant planet not entirely unlike my own planet insofar as it was obviously a hell of a lot more sophisticated than this weeping bedsore known as "The Earth"—still drank there, as did The Smooch. The Smooch hadn't changed any. He was still the same hardened, embittered ex-convict who had been incarcerated for vehicular homicide. Same leather jacket. Same torn dungarees. Same aviator sunglasses. Same everything.

Poor guy. The things he'd suffered! It was a miracle that he was still with us, that he hadn't hung himself yet in a fit of despair....

Arielle, I didn't see anymore. Raymond told me that Arielle had fallen head over heels for a lesbian survivalist, and that she was now living somewhere in The Ozarks with a bunch of other chain-smoking lesbian survivalists.

"What—is it supposed to be some kind of weird, post-apocalyptic commune or something?" I said to Raymond when he mentioned The Ozarks.

"Yeah. Something like that," Raymond replied.

"Yeah. It's really fucked up," interjected Murray. "I give her five weeks. Six—tops."

"And then what happens after six weeks?" I said.

"She comes crawling back here on her hands and knees, Franklin. Drives a cab again. Drinks boiler makers."

"Well, you just might be right about that."—That was Raymond now, agreeing with Murray.

"Guaranteed, Ray. I'll put money on it."

I, too, was inclined to agree with Murray.

**

Back on the home front, my impeccably moral & just father, who lit votive candles on Friday evenings in strict observance of the Jewish Sabbath, was becoming ever increasingly annoyed with me. Dad forbade me from using the car anymore for my mysterious excursions into The Isle of Manhattan.

"You want travel into Manhattan, Franklin? You want to hang out with 'artistic' people, do ya?" my father said to me one somber evening just before I was about to make like Houdini and do my usual nocturnal vanishing act.

"Who said anything about 'artistic' people, Dad?"

My father ignored the question and then repeated himself.

"You want to hang out with 'artistic' people, do you? With 'the intelligentsia?' Then take the train in."

"But the train is dangerous, Dad."

"Well, then take the bus in."

"But the bus is expensive, Dad. It's really expensive. And it doesn't run very often either."

"WHAT THE HELL DO I CARE HOW EXPENSIVE THE BUS IS OR HOW OFTEN IT RUNS! THAT AIN'T MY PROBLEM. I GOT MY OWN PROBLEMS."

"Well, what should I do then?"

"GET A JOB, FRANK. GET A *GOOD* JOB. NOT SOME SHIT JOB WORKING FOR DOUBLEDAY. THEN YOU CAN BUY YOUR OWN CAR AND DRIVE ALL OVER THE COUNTRY WITH IT."

I had been wondering how long it was going to take Dad to wise up. To start smelling the proverbial coffee and put his foot down on the old car keys.

Well, now I knew. The mystery was solved.

My father glared at me. It was very unsettling.

My mother added: "This business of coming home at 3 o'clock in the morning has got to stop, Franklin. It's extremely psychotic. What the hell do you do with yourself all night long, anyway?"

"I hang out at the library, Ma. I go to bookstores."

"At *that* hour?"

"Well, yeah. I study there. I drink coffee."

My mother rolled her eyes and walked out of the room. My father, too. My father turned on the television set.

"Well, that was easy enough," I thought to myself. "I wonder what goodies Ma has tucked away inside of the old ice box."

I walked over to the refrigerator and opened up the old ice box. There was a pint of vanilla ice cream inside of it and a couple of Oreo ice cream cookies. I picked up an Oreo ice cream cookie and then proceeded to tear off its plastic wrapper. I ate it. I liked it. I ate another one. I liked that one, too.

***

My life was becoming progressively unmanageable. The doorman of the building—Roberto—an extremely affable and intuitive fellow who sensed immediately that I wasn't myself, tried to buoy my waning spirits with the following sage piece of spiritual advice:

"Just get laid, Frank," Roberto counseled me. "Get a hand job. Get a blow job. Fuck your brains out. But don't pay for it!"

"Don't worry, Roberto. I won't. It'll be a cold day in Hell before Franklin Cohen has to pay for it."

"At a boy, Frank! That's the spirit! NOW GO OUT THERE AND GET SOME PUSSY, SOLDIER! That's an order!"

"Yes, sir!"

I saluted Roberto and then marched off to battle.

Another time Roberto said to me: "You know what's missing from your life, Franklin?"

"No, Roberto. What's missing from it?"

"Good old sunshine. Vitamin D."

"Is that so? So you think I'm Vitamin D deficient, huh?"

"Exactly!" exclaimed Roberto. "You need to get out more. Go to the beach or something."

"The beach, huh?"

"Yeah. The ocean. Do you like the ocean, Frank?"

"Yeah, I love the ocean."

"Me, too. I can't get enough of it. You've got your pussy there, and you've got your sunshine."

"And you've got your waves, too. Right?"

"Right."

Then Roberto said to me:

"You know, we should go to the beach some time, you and me. Have you been to the beach yet?"

"No, not this summer, Roberto."

"Well, we should go then! We should definitely go there. You want to go there?"

"Well... sure."

"At a boy, Frank! That's the spirit!"

"Well, when do you want to go exactly?"

"Soon, Frank."

"How soon?"

"I'll keep you posted."

"Yeah, you do that, Roberto."

Roberto reiterated at that point that he would definitely keep me posted about it.

And then he started going on again about the beach—about all of the sunshine and all of the Vitamin D and all of the great pussy there—especially the pussy.

Needless to say, Roberto and I never actually went to the beach together. Maybe Roberto did—by himself—but he never mentioned it to me and I never asked him about it.

***

All summer long I hung out in my room. I read stuff—porno, mostly—and I masturbated to kill time. My favorite pornographic magazine was a little number called *Jugs*. The photographs were taken in black & white, and they were printed on the shittiest newspaper you could imagine. However, I still found them extremely stimulating—considerably more so than the photos taken in your so-called "classier" mags such as *Playboy, Penthouse, Hustler*, etcetera. Phony women. All phony! Airbrushed into oblivion. Real women weren't airbrushed. They had moles. Imperfections. One breast was sometimes larger than the other breast, or hung down more than the other did. They had scars—from C-sections. They had stretch marks. Real women.

Sometimes, late at night, I could hear the couple who lived directly above us. The wife, a bleached blond. The husband, a corrections officer. Smoked cigars. El Productos. Always stunk up the entire building. Roberto had once bragged to me that he had had sexual intercourse with Mrs. Corrections Officer. Which I seriously doubted—knowing Roberto. Roberto would often brag to me about his various conquests since becoming a doorman. He would commence the bragging with the eighth & highest floor, and then he would continue the bragging with each of the lower floors; stopping only when he had reached the basement. According to Roberto, there were many, many HOT ladies who owned apartment shares within the cooperative, and they were all very very very FRUSTRATED. Roberto would then commence describing every single one of these HOT ladies in meticulous, exquisite detail. He would describe their moles. He would describe their scars. How much hair they had in their most intimate regions. You know.... Stuff like that. Important stuff. Roberto could go on all day about it.

***

Now: At the same time that I was hanging out with my good buddy, Roberto X. and learning all about my Vitamin D deficiency, I started re-reading what is probably my favorite book in the entire universe right after *Humboldt's Gift* by Saul Bellow and *Factotum* by Charles Bukowski entitled: *Endurance: Shackleton's Incredible Voyage*. This one was about the famous explorer's ill-fated expedition to reach The South Pole in the winter of 1914. My father always seemed to have plenty of books lying around on famous explorers and famous mountain climbers. Hunters.... Deep sea divers.... The scientists who worked on The Manhattan Project.... My father was just crazy about these "larger than life" types of characters. Read about 'em all the time. I, too, was crazy about 'em— particularly Shackleton. I just loved Shackleton. Couldn't seem to get enough of the guy. For anybody who is into famous explorers, or into stories about incredible feats of survival, then Sir Ernest Shackleton is definitely *the* guy. Not just a man, mind you. Something bigger. Something *much* bigger. A giant. A titan. A colossus. A demi-god. He was like Hercules. He was like Prometheus. He was like Beethoven— especially Beethoven. He was like Beethoven's Fifth Symphony or his *Appassionata* incarnate. Energy. Primal energy. The Life Force in its purest form. This type of primal energy is something which we urban dwellers have largely forgotten about—what with all of our creature comforts and mood-altering psychiatric "happy pills." But—rest assured—it is still in us. It is still in us and it is still all around us.

Some things truly are eternal.

After I had finished reading—and then *re*-reading for like... the twentieth or the thirtieth time—the account of that incredible voyage; and then of that *subsequent* incredible voyage from Elephant Island to South Georgia Island in a lifeboat called *The James Cairn*; I started re-reading yet another great book called *Annapurna* by Maurice Herzog. Then, after I had finished re-reading *Annapurna*, I started to re-read *View From The Summit: The Remarkable Memoir By The First Person To Conquer Everest*. And then finally, after re-reading Hillary's memoir, I started to re-read a macabre little gem about a group of unusually bloodthirsty man-eating tigers called *Man Eaters Of The Indus*. This one was extremely funny. Men—mostly stupid Englishmen—would daintily tip-toe like ballerinas about the fertile jungles of the Indus River basin, hoping to track down and then to capture a few of the man-eating Indus tigers. The man-eating Indus tigers, however—unlike the mostly stupid

Englishmen—knew better than to try to outsmart Nature. During the day they would hide deep in the jungle, killing time by reading *The Brothers Karamazov*; and then when night fell—under cover of darkness—they would suddenly re-emerge from their various hiding places and tear the mostly stupid Englishmen into little pieces. The mostly stupid Englishmen would always die. They would always die agonizing, brutal deaths because the mostly stupid Englishmen would always over-estimate their own extremely limited human intelligence and would always *under*-estimate the intelligence of animals.

I liked that one the best—the one about the man-eating Indus tigers.

***

One day—during the month of August—my College Boards-fixated, Harvard University-fixated, Medical School-fixated, monomaniacal, demented mother—who had slowly but surely been losing even more of her polluted marbles ever since I had politely informed her that NYU and I were now Splitsville—made an unexpected, surprise visit to her son's sleeping chamber, i.e., The Bastion Of Certitude. I had just then been finishing up a very interesting and unusual article in The Smithsonian Magazine entitled *In The Realms of the Unreal: The Mysterious Case Of Henry Darger*, when my mother suddenly burst into the beloved Bastion—extremely agitated—hysterical, even—and started ranting and raving about my apparently aberrant, abnormal lifestyle.

"My 'lifestyle'?" I said to my mother.

"Yes. Your lifestyle," my mother said to me.

"Well... what about my 'lifestyle'?"

"It's not normal," she said. "It's psychotic," she said. "It's perverted," she said. "It's DISEASED," she said.

"Well, what exactly makes it DISEASED?" I said.

"You know," she said.

"No, I don't know," I said. "You'll have to tell me, Ma. I'm not a mind reader."

"I mean your demeanor."

"My demeanor...."

"Your appearance."

"My appearance...."

"Your grooming."

"My *grooming?*"

"Yes, your grooming. Your personal hygiene. I mean... when was the last time you shaved, Franklin?"

"Gee, I don't know, Ma. A week ago maybe. Ten days...."

"TEN DAYS!"

"Yeah. Ten days. I mean I do have this weird skin condition."

"What weird skin condition?"

"It's called pseudofolliculitis barbae."

"Pseudofolliculitis what?"

"Barbae," I said.

"What's that?"

"It's a skin condition. It's a medically documented skin condition."

"I've never heard of that skin condition."

"Well, that's because you're not a dermatologist. Because if you were one, you would have."

"Is that so?"

"Yes. It is so."

"Well, what kind of a condition is it exactly?"

"I already told you."

"No, you didn't."

"It's razor bumps."

"What?"

"Razor bumps—a common condition of the beard area occurring in up to 60% of African-Americans."

"But you're not an African-American, dear!"

"Yes. I know, Ma. What a shock! However, pseudofolliculitis barbae can affect Caucasian people as well as Negroes. In fact, *anyone* who shaves their body hair on a regular basis can potentially acquire it."

"Can I, too, potentially acquire it?"

"Well, I don't see why not, Ma."

"I don't believe you."

I shrugged my shoulders then but kept my mouth shut. If Ma didn't want to believe that she, too, was susceptible to razor burn, then that was just fine by me. I mean... it was her body. Her body hair. Her razor burn. Her stupidity.

Never argue with a stupid person. It's a waste of time; you'll never get anywhere. Only argue with intelligent people because intelligent people will always agree with you—which is precisely what makes them so intelligent. You don't believe me? Well, see for yourself then. Try arguing with a thousand stupid people. In fact, try arguing with *ten thousand* stupid people. And then get back to me. We'll have a good laugh.

"Well, even if you do have this Barbie Doll skin condition—"

"—I do, and it's not a Barbie Doll."

"—Well, whatever it is, you're still missing the point, Frank."

"Which is?"

"You know damned well what the point is. I'm talking about your physical appearance. About your *mental demeanor*. About the way that you—Franklin Horatio Archibald Cohen—choose to present yourself to the real world."

"The real world, huh?"

"Yeah. Correct."

"Okay, Ma. Fair enough. Only before continuing with your insightful analysis of my abnormal, psychotic, perverted 'lifestyle,' would you mind telling me what that is exactly?"

"What *what* is exactly?"

"This mysterious 'real world' that you're always talking about."

"Oh, please, Frank. Don't play games with me."

"Who's playing games, Ma? It's a legitimate question."

"No, Frank. It's a stupid question."

"Well... *to you* maybe it's a stupid question, but not to me, Ma. To me it's a great one. Does it mean, say... getting up every morning and taking the train in to go to work along with all of the other domesticated, expendable farm animals? Being an exceedingly docile, obedient farm animal and getting a pat on the head for it in the form of a 'paycheck?' Paying all sorts of compulsory taxes on it? Paying Federal taxes? Paying State taxes? Paying City taxes? Paying sales taxes? Paying property taxes? Self-employment taxes? Capital gains taxes? Estate taxes? Being trapped in a monopolistic—essentially totalitarian—financial system in which huge, megalithic banks are allowed to print funny money whenever they feel like it? Out of thin air? Out of *nothing?* And which is backed by nothing other than some government decree which *says* that it's worth something—which it really isn't, of course. Hey. If *they* can do it, then why can't *we* do it? I mean... if I want to buy a house, for instance, only I don't have a dime to my name to buy it with, then why can't I buy it *anyway* just by writing the owner a worthless check and then saying to the guy: 'Trust me. This is worth something. You have my word on it. Now hand over the fucking keys, asshole.' Is that what you mean, Ma? Is that what you're talking about? The world of funny money? The world of monopoly money? The world of worthless, value-less pieces of toilet paper?"

My mother stared at me then—she stared at me HARD—as if I were some kind of odious bug or something. Like I was a cockroach. Like I was a dung beetle. Like I was some kind of crazy, lunatic-fringe conspiracy theorist who was suddenly pissing on the very bedrock of her precious Norman Rockwell American wet dream. "Get away from me, you crazy nut you! With your crazy, lunatic-fringe conspiracy theories. Leave Norman and me the hell alone!" That sort of hard stare. Then, after she had finished staring at me—after she had finished gazing at me in abject horror—she said to me in a sorrowful voice:

"Tell me, son. What seems to be troubling you?"

"Why, nothing at all, Ma. What makes you say that?"

"Well, there has to be *something*," she said. "Some *reason*. I mean...

this doesn't just suddenly... *happen*."

"WHAT doesn't just suddenly happen?"

"You know...."

"NO, I DON'T KNOW!

My mother shook her head then very slowly—exceedingly slowly—with her two un-seeing eyes closed; and then she turned her disappointed, sorrowful countenance up to the heavens above her—or, in this case, the ceiling above her. I assumed that she was communing with God—asking The Good Lord to grant her the serenity to deal with stupid assholes like her idiot offspring.

The Good Lord said something to her then—I don't know what exactly— but something marvelous. Something really awe-inspiring and worthy of Yahweh... like: "Don't you worry, you saintly woman you. You Mother Theresa you. You Eleanor Roosevelt you. Take heart, Doris. Don't despair. We'll make a *mensch* out of The Asshole yet."

"Really, Lord? You're not just saying that?"

"No, Dotty. I'm not just saying that."

"Well, then what should I do, Lord? I mean... what's the game plan?"

"The game plan? Very simple. Just keep doing what you're doing, Dotty. Keep hammering away at him. Go for the body shots. Eventually you'll wear him down to the point where all he can think about is becoming a doctor—or if not a doctor, then an orthodontist; or if not an orthodontist, then a corporate attorney; or if not a corporate attorney, then a CPA. How's that grab ya, Dotty—his becoming an accountant?"

"Sounds good, Lord!"

"Okay. Terrific. I'll make a note of it then in My Celestial Calendar: 'Get The Shit Head to go to Business School.'"

"Gee, thanks, Lord!

"Hey, no problem."

And then The Good Lord politely excused Himself to attend to His other affairs, which were multitudinous.

5. GOD'S PROMISE FULFILLED

In the fall of 1976—on a beautiful Indian summer's morning—with a beautiful sky just above me, and a magnificent city all around me save for those few, isolated, rare pockets of *un*-magnificence and rampant squalor—I started taking accounting classes at Fordham University Business School at its newly-constructed Manhattan campus. I was 23 years old at the time and I was an alien from another planet. From a far-away, distant galaxy where the inhabitants didn't kill each other. Didn't lie. Didn't cheat. Didn't steal. Weren't dishonorable. Didn't spend literally their entire lives—from cradle to grave—being the obedient slaves of a tyrannical system which treated them all as if they were dumb farm animals. As if they were docile sheep. As if they were expendable livestock. Question: What do you do with an obedient slave who doesn't realize that he's an obedient slave? Who thinks he's happy? Contented? Well adjusted? *Fulfilled?* And the answer: Not much. There's really nothing much that you can do with him. You can try *telling* the obedient slave, of course, that he's really just an obedient slave. Explaining it to him. Breaking it down for him. Putting it to him in the simplest of terms. Only watch out, Promethean Fire-Giver! Be on your guard, Fire-Giver. Be eternally vigilant. Because if you don't explain it to the slave properly—if you come on too strong—or not strong enough—you just might find yourself at the end of a rope.

Anyway, there I was. I was an alien from another planet who was trying to impersonate a human being. Who was trying to impersonate a college graduate—some dewy-eyed, dreamy English major who was currently unemployed in a failing economy. The dewy-eyed, dreamy English major had a crazy father and an even crazier mother who were constantly, forever pressuring him to "do something" with his sorry life—until finally, as a result of the pressuring—of the constant needling, and of the constant whining, and of the constant bitching, and of the constant moaning—he had consented—albeit reluctantly—to taking a couple of lousy, stinking, boring Accounting courses.

Pretty good disguise, huh?—pretending to be some dewy-eyed, dreamy English major who couldn't really do very much of anything other than read books and brood in his bedroom. Not to toot my own horn or anything, but in my opinion it was a lot sneakier than any "sneaky" question on some fake, practice test. Took me a while, though, to come up with it. Originally, I had been toying with the idea of trying to impersonate one of the so-called "Beautiful People." You know.... One of The Chosen Few. One of The Gilded Ones. The latest "flavor of the month" celebrity air-head who everybody is always talking about. You see them on TV, in the movies, on billboards, in fashion magazines. Those kinds of "Beautiful People." The only problem, however, with the so-called "Beautiful People"—aside, that is, from the rather lamentable fact that their sudden, meteoric rise to fame is usually based on nothing more than blatant nepotism—is that they are often exceedingly empty-headed, clueless creatures. In fact, *most* celebrities are of this particular ilk. They actually believe all of the bull shit that comes with celebrity. All of the platitudes.... All of the lies.... And once you start going down that road paved with Fool's Gold, it's basically over. You're basically washed up. Whatever talent you once had is now obliterated by all of the bull shit; and whatever integrity you once had, now replaced by unrelenting self-loathing. Endless days of it and endless nights. No. *No!* Better to be a "nobody," I thought to myself. Better to be anonymous— one of the unwashed, teeming masses. At least that way I could freely circulate. Freely maneuver myself. Freely investigate without being weighed down by some massive ego. Yes. There was a lot to be said for "The Anonymous Lifestyle." It had a lot going for it. True: It wasn't very flashy or very noisy or very messy like "The Celebrity Lifestyle" was. But it got the job done. It did it marvelously.

Remember: David didn't kill Goliath by using his overwhelming, overpowering charisma. He killed him just by using a simple stone.

Something to think about when you meet your next Goliath.

***

One day while I was sitting in my Accounting class, pretending to be extremely interested in all of the intricacies of Cost Accounting—that most fascinating of all subjects—I spied a woman—not unlike myself— who seemed to share my intense passion for the quasi-miraculous world of Profit & Loss. Then I saw her the next day. And then the next day. And then the next day. And then the next one—until finally—after the sixth day—I decided that it was high time to approach this mysterious woman and to introduce myself as a fellow accounting lover.

"Hi, there," I said to the woman. "My name is Franklin Cohen. What's your name?"

"Sandy Scorzo."

"Well hi, Sandy!"

"Hi, Franklin."

"Pleased to meet cha!"

"Yeah. Likewise."

"So… why the heck are you studying Cost Accounting at Lincoln Center, if you don't mind my asking you?"

"No. I don't mind your asking me," this Sandy Scorzo person replied.

"Well, why then?"

"Well… why not? I mean… what's wrong with studying Cost Accounting?"

"Why, nothing at all, Sandy," I replied. "I think that studying Cost Accounting is a perfectly admirable pursuit—just as long as it doesn't involve child molestation."

"Excuse me? I didn't catch that."

"I said that studying Cost Accounting is just terrific—provided, of course, that you're the type of person who enjoys water torture or electrocution."

"And you don't?"

"No, not really."

"Well, what are *you* doing studying Cost Accounting then?"

"Me?" I replied.

"Yeah. You."

"Well, you see I'm not really studying Cost Accounting, Sandy."

"Oh, no?"

"No."

"Then what are you doing here?"

"Studying humans."

"Excuse me?"

"I said studying humanity."

"Studying humanity?"

"Yeah, that's my real objective—not this mind-numbing Accounting bull shit. You see, Sandy, I'm really an alien from another planet who has been sent to The Earth on a secret mission."

"Secret mission?"

"Yes."

"What kind of a 'mission'?"

"An extra-terrestrial, intergalactic one."

"For what purpose?"

"Well, I just told you the purpose."

"To study humanity?"

"Yes. To study humanity."

At that point Sandy smiled at me—sort of. It was very similar to the way you might smile at some obviously deranged, psychotic person. You know.... Some escaped mental patient who you were trying to humor until the men in the white coats finally got there. Or maybe it was that kind of a "knowing" smile which betrays a tremendous amount of furtive admiration. Or *maybe* it was even that kind of a "knowing smile" which seemed to be saying: "Well, I certainly applaud you on your noble efforts, Alien; only... take it from a fellow Alien who's already been on exactly the same, identical mission: there is absolutely nothing at all to be learned here. It's just another barren rock. Abort, abort."

It was *that* kind of a smile—sort of. An ambiguous smile. An enigmatic smile. And since you now know what a softee I am for everything which is enigmatic; for everything which is complex; ambiguous; subtle; and fraught with double meanings; I don't think that it will come as much of a shock to you when I tell you that I felt pretty good about having decided to talk to Sandy.

Is this the star that I seek? I thought to myself. This materialization of it? This *incarnation* of it? Maybe, I thought to myself. *Maybe....* This practical joke is just full of surprises.

Presently, The Ambiguous One said to me—donning once again her "*un*-ambiguous" robes:

"And just where exactly is your planet located, Franklin?"

"Well, are you at all familiar with Orion, Sandy?"

"You mean Orion The Hunter? The constellation?"

"That's right. The constellation."

"Well... yeah. Sure. I mean, who doesn't know Orion The Hunter?"

"Oh, you'd be surprised, Sandy. There are lots of people. Looking up at the night sky and studying the stars is practically a dead art. Most humans can no longer do it."

"Well, the Vikings could do it."

"Yes, the Vikings could do it. The Egyptians.... The Greeks.... The Sumerians.... The Babylonians.... The Mayans.... The Phoenicians.... The Persians.... The ancient Hebrews.... But they're all dead now—those ancient star gazers. Now it's all about *Star Trek* and *Star Wars*—watching imaginary shoot-'em-ups in a movie theater where Outer Space is the new Wild West."

"Yes, that's true, Franklin" Sandy said. "I suppose we do seem to have less and less of them."

"I mean... you still have your 'official' star gazers, of course, in the form of professional astronomers and astrophysicists. The Arecibo radio telescope, for example, located in The Commonwealth of Puerto Rico, and its search for extra-terrestrial signs of intelligence.... The Hubble telescope.... The whole insane 'race to the moon' thing.... But that's a completely different animal. The 'professional star gazer.' Who makes a living doing it. Wouldn't you agree, Sandy?"

"In what way?"

"Well, in this way: Broadcasting encoded messages to some remote star cluster in the constellation Hercules in an attempt to find out whether you're alone in the universe is all very well and good, I suppose. But this is a very highly specialized kind of 'star gazing' which the average person is totally removed from. The average person couldn't give a flying fuck that it really only takes Mercury fifty-nine Earth days to make one full rotation about its axis and not eighty-nine, as was previously thought. No, I'm not talking about that kind of thing. I'm talking about something else here. I'm talking about a kind of generalized 'stellar consciousness' which the ancients were obviously in acute possession of; but which you modern Earthlings seem to have lost completely."

"Well, what exactly have we lost, Franklin?"

"Why, you've lost The Forest, of course. The Big Picture. You can see the trees now very clearly, Sandy, but there's no more Forest. There are just... *many forests*."

"Oh, I see," she said. "Oh, that's very clever."

"Oh, but I'm not trying to be 'clever,' Sandy. I'm just stating the obvious: Your world founders."

"And yours doesn't?"

"What?"

"Founder."

"Well.... Let me put it to you this way, Sandy. We, too, are not without our... problems. Oh, we have many problems. Many 'weak spots.' Only *our* 'weak spots' are different than yours are. I mean, we handle them differently. We approach them differently. We don't try to 'cover them up'—the way you humans do—by constantly drowning ourselves in a sea of data. Data is meaningless unless it lifts The Spirit."

"And just where exactly is your planet again?"

"Oh, it's far away, Sandy."

"How far?"

"Over a thousand light years."

"Where exactly?"

"Well, that's the reason why I originally asked you if you were at all familiar with Orion The Hunter. You see, if you go to the middle star in Orion's belt—"

"—You come from *there*, Franklin?"

"No. Not exactly. You go to the middle star in Orion's belt, and then you hang a left at the first traffic light. Then you go straight again—past the asteroids—and make another left at the black hole. You can't miss it. It's a blue planet."

"What's it called, Franklin?"

"It's called Malinla."

"Come again?"

"I said Malinla."

"Spell it for me, will ya?"

"Yeah, sure. It's spelled M-A-L-I-N-L-A. Malinla."

"Well, that's an odd name."

"Well, maybe in English it is. But in our language it's a beautiful name."

"Well, what exactly does it mean, Franklin?"

"Oh, many things. Many noble things. It has all sorts of subtle meanings depending upon the way you use it."

"Like what, for example? Give me one of the meanings."

"Well, one of the meanings—loosely translated of course—would be something like... 'He who continually fails at something, but who tries so doggedly to succeed at it so that even his failure is a kind of raving success.' Or maybe: 'He who tries to do something which is damned near impossible to do.' Or maybe: 'What he lacks in talent, he tries to make up for with hard work.' Or maybe even something as corny and trite—but at the same time profoundly beautiful—as: 'If at first you don't succeed, try try try again.' Something like that, anyway. I think you get the idea."

"So Malinla really means 'failure,' huh?"

"Well, no. Not really 'failure' per se. Because whenever you humans use the word 'failure,' it always has all of these negative connotations. It connotes incompetence. Or moral weakness. Or maybe just a shockingly 'immature,' muddled nature. You know…. 'Hey, Sam. Get a load of Fred over there. What a failure, right? What a born loser. I mean… the guy comes from a really well-connected, wealthy family…. Goes to all of the right schools…. Is introduced to all of the right people…. And what does 'knuckle head' decide to do after he finally graduates from his 'right' college? He decides to chuck it all by becoming a 'writer.' Can you believe it, Sam? *A fucking writer!* Do you see what I'm saying, Sandy?"

"Yes, I see exactly what you're saying, Franklin."

"No, the term 'Malinla' isn't at all like that."

"So… Malinla is a *good* thing then?"

"Oh, it's a very beautiful, amazing thing. To say that a sentient being is 'Malinla' is the highest honor which we can bestow upon it. It's not like *your* honors. Our honors actually *mean* something. You see, we don't have any 'Nobel Peace Prizes,' or 'Freedom Of Thought Gold Medals,' or 'Honorary Degrees For Distinguished Services Rendered To Mankind.' Those awards are merely 'window dressing'—concocted by clever people with clever bank accounts in order to reassure the public that moral order prevails. Prevails my ass! I mean…. My goodness, Sandy…. With all of these outstanding humanitarian awards, and philanthropic awards, and awards for Freedom Of Thought, and for Distinguished Services Rendered To Mankind, and so and so forth, etcetera, etcetera which you hypocritical human beings are so enamoured of bestowing upon one another… why, you'd think that The

Earth was some kind of Garden Of Eden instead of the reptilian shit hole which it really is. So many dedicated, noble people doing so many altruistic, noble things...."

"So I take it then that you 'Malinlians' aren't particularly bowled over by us human beings, are you?"

"No, Sandy. Not particularly."

"Well, is there *anybody* on our planet who your own planet isn't repulsed by?"

"As a matter of fact, Sandy, there is. There are a few rare, notable exceptions."

"Oh, well that's very big of you, Franklin."

"Thanks. But you have to remember something, Miss Scorzo—is it Miss Scorzo or is it Mrs. Scorzo?"

"It's Miss Scorzo—*Ms.*, actually."

"Ah.... But you have to remember something, *Ms.* Scorzo. These few rare, notable exceptions bear absolutely no resemblance to the rest of humanity. I mean... sure. They have ten fingers and ten toes, and two eyes and two ears, and two arms and two legs, and a pair of lungs, and a pair of kidneys and so forth—but that's pretty much where the resemblance ends. You see, these rare exceptions which I am referring to are truly the one-in-a-billion 'freaks' of humanity. You want to talk about 'miracles,' Sandy? Well then, these are the *real* miracles—these freakish anomalies. I mean, *these* anomalies really existed. They were actually *real people—with real lives*—unlike those larger-than-life heavenly Houdinis whose miraculous deeds are more a matter of faith than they are of fact. Your own Beethoven, for example, would be the most notable of these 'freakish anomalies'."

"You mean Beethoven—the composer?"

"Yes, that's right. Beethoven—the composer. Beethoven is the perfect example of a sentient being who defines Malinla—which is precisely why we have decided to name our planet Planet Beethoven—in honor of Beethoven."

"Hey, wait a minute there, buster."

"What?"

"Didn't you just say that the planet you come from is called 'Planet Malinla?'"

"Oh, it is, Sandy. It is. But it can also be called 'Planet Beethoven' because 'Beethoven' and 'Malinla' mean exactly the same thing in our language."

"Okay. So let me get this straight, Franklin...."

"Yes?"

"'Malinla' doesn't just mean one thing. It can mean *many* things."

"Why, that's exactly right, Ms. Scorzo."

"So let's say—just for argument's sake—that there's this... place on this 'reptilian shit hole of ours,' as you so magnanimously deign to call our planet, which is known as Papua New Guinea."

"Yes, I have heard of Papua New Guinea. They eat people there, do they not?"

"Well, not so much anymore, Franklin. Nowadays the inhabitants of Papua New Guinea would probably prefer drinking coffee at Starbucks. You know. Cappuccinos.... Double lattes.... Frappuccinos with extra chocolate sauce. That sort of thing."

"Frappuccinos? Extra chocolate sauce?"

"Never mind, Franklin. Skip it. Anyway—just for clarity's sake—let's suppose—hypothetically speaking now—that the inhabitants of Papua New Guinea suddenly arrive at the realization—after thousands & thousands of years of murdering people and then making hamburgers and link sausages out of them—that maybe—just *maybe*—they ought to look elsewhere for a source of nourishment. Instead of butchering their fellow man and making hamburgers and link sausages out of him, they decide to become vegetarians. Cultivate gardens. Grow tomatoes. Grow soybeans. Eat tofu. And whenever they find themselves hankering for a nice, juicy human hamburger or for a nice, juicy link sausage made out of the latest missionary who wants to convert them; they simply channel those primitive cravings of theirs into painting. Or writing. Or pottery. Or sculpting. Or maybe volunteering once a week at their local animal shelter or Suicide Hotline. So... I guess what I'm trying to ask you is this: would you or would you not agree with me that this radical shift in the Papua New Guinea lifestyle from one of cannibalism to that of veganism would be a manifestation of your Malinla?"

"Oh, I would absolutely agree with you, Sandy, that it would be a manifestation of our Malinla. That's an absolutely spot-on, stellar analogy. *Or*—were you so inclined—you could also put it to me in the following manner: that the inhabitants of Papua New Guinea have now finally—at long last—reached a sufficiently elevated level of consciousness so that they can begin to gravitate towards Malinla. Or so that they can begin to concentrate on Malinla. Or so that they can begin to partake of Malinla. Or so that they can begin to drink from The Eternal Wellspring and Forever Nexus of The God Malinla (which is also, of course, The Eternal Wellspring and Forever Nexus of The God Beethoven). Something like that, anyway. But I think you've got it."

"Give me another one, will you, Frank."

"Another what?"

"Another example."

"But you just gave me a perfectly lovely one."

"Not good enough."

"Not *good* enough?"

"No. I feel that we need an even *better* example."

"Well, what do you have in mind exactly?"

"Well, you tell me, Frank. I mean... it's *your* concept."

"What is?"

"You know.... Malinla."

I thought about it for a couple of seconds. Sandy was right. We *could* do better. As a matter of fact, we could do *a lot* better. After all, Malinla was an exceedingly slippery concept. It wasn't like greed, or lust, or anger, or duplicity. These concepts the humans could grasp. They were simple concepts to suit a simple species. However, Malinla wasn't. And *we* weren't. We were better than that. More advanced than that. It takes a stone many centuries in order to become worn smooth by the elements. It takes hundreds of years. Sometimes thousands, even. And the spirit of man is much more obdurate than stone is.

"Alright, Sandy," I said to her presently. "You want an even *better* example? Well, here then. Here's an even *better* example."

"Oh, goody!" she said. "An even *better* example!"

"Let's say, Sandy—just for argument's sake—that your mother is an old hag."

"Excuse me?"

"I said an old hag. You know…. A demon. A witch. A sorceress. A she-devil."

"Okay. I got it now. So my mother is an old hag."

"No. Not your mother. *My* mother."

"No—you got it right the first time."

"Okay then. *Our* mothers. *Our* mothers are old hags. Well, you and I now have a decision to make."

"What decision?"

"Oh, a very important decision. You see, at this point, now that we've finally come to accept the fact—after many, many fruitless years of trying to squeeze blood out of a block of marble, and to extract precious metals out of pile of horse manure—that our respective mothers are indeed old hags; you and I can either make the fateful decision to continue struggling with our respective old hags; OR—"

"—Well, what do you mean by 'continue struggling with'?"

"You know…. Continue arguing with. Continue *pleading with*. Continue screaming at. Continue turning blue in the face over. In short, continue trying to get them to change their 'hag' natures into beautiful natures. Into *nurturing* natures."

"Okay. Gotcha. I understand now. Sounds familiar. Sounds *very* familiar."

"OR—and here's where it gets interesting, Sandy—we can decide *not* to continue struggling with them. To *refuse* to continue struggling with them."

"Well, what do we do then if we refuse to continue struggling with them?"

"We withdraw, Sandy. We *retreat*."

"Retreat where, Frank?"

"Into The Bastion Of Certitude."

"The Bastion Of Certitude?"

"Yeah. Exactly."

"And just where exactly is this 'Bastion' located, Franklin?"

"Oh, I think you know, Sandy. I think you know very well where The Bastion is located."

Sandy considered my comment for a few measured seconds. And as she did so—once again—I seemed to discern the same faintly ambiguous, enigmatic, "knowing" smile beginning mischievously to re-emerge from out of the corners of her thin lips. What silver linings are to opaque clouds; so, too, are obvious answers to disingenuous questions.

"Oh. You mean *that* place?" she said to me presently.

"That's right. *That* place," I answered her back. And then I added: "And if you do indeed decide to retreat into it—"

"Oh, what a lovely word!"

"What?"

"Retreat."

"Yes. I suppose it is a lovely word, come to think of it."

"It's so calming. So reassuring. To know that there's this... special place which you can always go to in order to think in peace. Without being constantly bothered."

"Well, I guess that's why they call it 'a retreat,' huh?"

Sandy nodded. She really liked the word.

"Anyway, Sandy.... Like I was just saying: If you do indeed decide to retreat into The Bastion—that is to say, to take the much-more-obscure, unfamiliar high road as opposed to the extremely visible, obvious, low one—well... then that, too, would be the kind of spiritual decision which we, on our world, would associate with Malinla Consciousness."

"Will you marry me, Franklin?"

"Excuse me?"

"I said: Will you marry me, Franklin."

"Well... Yeah. Sure, Sandy. I'll marry you."

"Oh, goody! He says yes!"

"Is that what you humans call 'a marriage proposal'?"

"Well, usually it's the male of the species who makes the proposal."

"I see."

"However, it isn't written in stone or anything. A woman can propose to a man too if she wants."

"I see, Sandy. Very interesting."

"So you'll do it then?"

"What?"

"Marry me."

"Affirmative, Sandy. I accept the proposal. Only... before we take the plunge, honeybun, only to wake up one dismal morning twenty years after the fact only to realize that we were never compatible, don't you think we should go on a date first? I mean, just to confirm that we're the perfect couple?"

"Why, that's an absolutely terrific idea, sweetheart!"

"Well, where do you live, Sandy?"

"I live in the Bronx, darling."

"Me, too! What a coincidence!"

"But didn't you just say that you lived on a planet a thousand light years away from The Earth?"

"I did indeed. Actually, it's a little over a thousand."

"So then what's all this about The Bronx, Frank? What—is The Bronx some kind of Malinla 'colony' or something?"

"Heaven forbid, Sandy! That would be awful. No—I'm just staying here temporarily with my designated, demented Earth parents until Commander O'Brien comes to collect me."

"Well, when is he coming, Frank?"

"Gee, I don't know, Sandy. Commander O'Brien didn't say exactly. It could be this week. It could be next week. It could be next month. Or it could be never."

"Do you really think he'll never show?"

"Well no, Sandy. That's highly unlikely. I mean, Commander O'Brien is an honorable person. If he says he'll show—then he's gonna show. Only it might take awhile. Several years, possibly. You know, Commander O'Brien is a very busy person, Sandy. He's got a lot on his mind. You know. Reports.... Deadlines.... Presentations.... Other missions...."

"You mean, you're not the only one?"

"Hell no! He's got like... a hundred missions going simultaneously."

"Gee. That's a lot of missions."

"Yeah. Tell me about it."

"So I guess it's true then."

"So you guess *what's* true then?"

"That you're really stuck here—at least for the time being, anyway."

"Yeah, I guess so. Lucky me, huh?"

"So... where exactly in the Bronx do *you* live, Frank?"

"In a magical place call RIVERDALE."

"Well then, we're practically neighbors because I live on Gun Hill."

"Do you really?"

"Yes. Really. Well... not actually on Gun Hill. I live on Bainbridge—near Gun Hill."

"I know where that is! That's right next to a cemetery. A big cemetery. What's it called again?"

"The Woodlawn Cemetery."

"Oh, yeah. Right. The Woodlawn Cemetery...."

Then, right after we'd finished discussing where in The Bronx we both lived, I asked Sandy for her phone number. She gave me a business card with her name printed on it:

SANDRA F. SCORZO - MANAGEMENT SPECIALIST

"Is that what you are?" I said. "A 'management specialist'?"

"Well, that's what companies who hire file clerks like to call 'em these days: management specialists. Now... there *used* to be time when, if you were a file clerk, then they'd call you a file clerk. But not anymore, Frank. Those days are long gone. Nowadays if you're simply a file clerk, you're really 'a management specialist' or 'a business associate.' It sounds better. More important."

"I see," I said. "More lies," I said. "And what exactly does the F stand for?"

"The F," she said, "stands for Faith."

"Well, that's a very pretty middle name, Sandy. It's like Elvira. Or Olivia. Or Angelica. Or Isadora. You don't hear those kinds of names much anymore."

"No, I guess not, Frank."

"It's honest and it's old fashioned—and I like honest and old fashioned. I'm very traditional, you know, Sandy. I hate phonies—*loathe* phonies."

"Yeah, I noticed, Frank. Me, too."

We made a date then for Saturday night. Sandy's place. Around seven-ish. We both agreed that if the date went well, that we would get married at Niagara Falls the following Tuesday by a Tibetan Lama—that is, if we could find one on short notice.

"Until Saturday then, Faith. May The Force be with you," I said to Sandy.

"Likewise," said Sandy.

Sandra Scorzo was an unusual person.

***

The following Saturday evening, at approximately 7 PM, I kept my hot date with Sandra Scorzo. Sandy hadn't been kidding me when she had said that the block she lived on overlooked a cemetery. It was a huge cemetery—The Woodlawn Cemetery—final resting place of such noted celebrities as: Rosa Parks, Aretha Franklin, Duke Ellington, Irving Berlin, Miles Davis, Lionel Hampton, Otto Preminger, and Bat Masterson. There were many other famous people, of course, who were buried in The Woodlawn Cemetery. Probably hundreds of 'em. Maybe thousands, even. Herman Melville is also buried there, the author of *Moby-Dick*. Yeah. That guy. His gravestone is a very simple affair. All that it says is:

HERMAN MELVILLE

Born August 1, 1819

Died September 28, 1891

That is all. There is nothing else.

Sandy's apartment building, on the other hand, in sharp contrast to The Woodlawn Cemetery, was totally uninspiring and underwhelming. It was just your typical pre-World War II apartment building built of red brick—eight stories high—no better and no worse than all of the other pre-World War II apartment buildings built of red brick which had been constructed there. All of these totally uninspiring, generic apartment buildings—the phrase "cookie-cutter" comes to mind here—were uniformly grimy and weather-beaten—just like the sea of headstones in the adjacent cemetery. Decades of soot and microscopic particulate matter had all but obliterated the building's original color—which had been a bright, merry, reddish brown. In fact, the weather-beaten, grimy brickwork no longer even resembled brickwork. It resembled something else—a kind of palimpsest—which had been written upon and then re-written upon many dozens of times over until the original manuscript was just a shadow—a pale ghost—of its former glory. In a funny way, it was almost beautiful—this incrementally slow erosive process which had been going on since the Thirties. You couldn't get that sort of distressed look by trying to create it in a deliberate fashion. It took time. It took lots of time. Nature will always be the best artist.

Sandy's apartment was on the sixth floor. There was an elevator but I took the stairs up. When I got to her floor, I stood in the hallway briefly, waiting for my labored breathing to subside—or at least to diminish to "acceptable" levels so that it couldn't possibly be misconstrued as being one of the classic symptoms of an acute anxiety attack—which it definitely wasn't because I wasn't anxious. I was feeling calm. I was feeling relaxed. I was feeling *very* relaxed—slightly euphoric, even. I was looking forward to my date with Sandy. It would be my first date with a female human and I was feeling extremely proud of myself for having made it. I was acting just like a regular person—and regular persons went out on dates, didn't they? They went out to dinner. They went to the movies. They went to museums. They went to bowling alleys. Oh, my superiors back on Planet Beethoven would have been absolutely delighted about this latest turn of events. A real date with a real human! And with an *intelligent* human! That was the kicker. "Good man, Corporal!" they would have all said to me. "Now we're getting somewhere! Now we're going places!!"

Yes.... There was a promotion for me in this somewhere, I felt—if only I could manage to complete my mission without drawing any undue attention to myself; write my report up while it was still fresh in my mind; and then get the hell out of this God-forsaken reptilian shit hole as soon as possible without being eaten alive.

***

We were sitting comfortably on Sandy's sofa. We were drinking "the good stuff"—the really "special stuff"—which you only cracked open on special occasions: the '67 Cabernet Sauvignon which Sandy's sister, Anabella, had given to her as a Christmas present. I had my left arm around Sandy and I was resting my right arm on a throw pillow. I was also using my left hand and my left fingers to play with Sandy's under-developed, girlish breasts; first feeling them very gently, then caressing them, and then squeezing them in a kind of "milking" or "massaging" fashion—a little something which I had picked up from another magazine called *Casabas*. While I was doing this, Sandy's eyes were closed. Sandy was very quiet—very intense looking—as if she were trying to solve some kind of high school math problem all in her head without using a pocket calculator, or a slide rule, or a pencil & paper—or anything—such as: "If Alpha Centauri is four light years away, and if the speed of light is 328,262 miles per second, and if our current technology only allows us to build rocket ships that can travel at the speed of 30,000 miles per hour, then how long would it take Man to...." That sort of high school math problem. And the fact that she was so deadly serious about it—so completely *into* the problem—so intent on "solving it" correctly—as if nothing less than the fate of the entire universe hung precariously in the balance—oh, I liked that! I liked it A LOT. How strange it was.... How *rare* it was.... The utter absorption in it. The utter commitment to it. The focus.... The concentration.... The stillness.... Ah, yes! *The stillness.* I mean... let's be brutally honest here, shall we? Just how often were any of these human beings—any of these feeble-minded, weak-willed, all-too-easily-distractable human beings—able to focus on anything—anything at all? Able to give it their total, undivided attention without becoming terminally, hopelessly bored after about... oh, I don't know... a half an hour, maybe? An hour, maybe? Two hours, maybe? An entire morning, maybe? That is to say, an entire morning, maybe, on a *good* day—on a really *great, amazing, colossal* day after they'd taken their daily dose of Ritalin or Adderall or Dexedrine or Concerta, and downed five or six double espressos. Now... bear in mind: When I put the question to you: "Just how often were any of these human beings—any of these feeble-minded, weak-willed, all-too-easily-distractable human beings—able to focus on anything—anything at all?" I'm not just talking about that kind of "bare bones," minimal focus you need in order to drag yourself out of bed in the morning, shower & shave, down some hot coffee, and then trudge begrudgingly into work. I mean... we all have to make sacrifices. We all have to show up for work in at least a semi-conscious, non-comatose condition, and then do whatever it is that our employers require of us in order to keep earning that Almighty Paycheck. No. I'm not talking about that kind of "focus." I'm talking about *real focus*. Real commitment. Being as serious about it as a heart attack. Doing the thing as if your life depended upon it—the lives of your children—the lives of your grandchildren. Not many of us are able to do that. In fact, very few of us are able to do that. We tend to do the things that we do only *half*-heartedly—not whole-heartedly. Some of us are incapable of whole-heartedness due to some kind of obvious physical and / or emotional infirmity; whereas still *others* among us who are incapable of whole-heartedness, are incapable of it due either to a tremendously overwhelming sense of cynicism; or else to a tremendously overwhelming sense of lassitude. Why cynicism, you ask? Why lassitude, you ask? Well, why *not* cynicism and why *not* lassitude? I mean... our entire society is currently based on the premise that the individual is totally irrelevant; and his aspirations, equally irrelevant if that individual and if those aspirations do not fully comport with the reigning Zeitgeist. If the reigning Zeitgeist happens to be sympathetic to socialism or to some other form of collectivism; then the individual, too, must embrace socialism or that other form of collectivism if he wishes to avoid being marginalized, or completely ignored altogether. And if the reigning Zeitgeist happens to be sympathetic to a vibrant, enterprising, pioneering spirit.... Well... actually... that almost never happens. The current Zeitgeist—whatever it may be—is almost always much more sympathetic to collectivism and to repression than it is to free enterprise and to the spirit of trail-blazing. But you get my point, right? Where is the individual in all of this? The individual, I say, is nowhere. The individual is completely lost in the shuffle. Hence, the individual's overwhelming cynicism. Hence, his lassitude. Hence, his hopelessness. And when you feel hopeless, you don't feel much like doing anything. Or if you *do* have to do something—I mean, if you really *have to* and if there's just no way of getting around it—then you don't put your heart into it. You do it half-assed—not *whole*-assed. Half-heartedly—not *whole*-heartedly. That's what happens to you when you become a slave to The Zeitgeist.

    Anyway.... The point is: that while human beings—for whatever reason—generally tend to do the things that they do in an extremely half-hearted, tepid manner; here was a creature—*a human being, no less!*—who was being uncustomarily *whole*-hearted. WHOLE-hearted, I say! Not half-hearted. Not quarter-hearted. Not an eighth-hearted. Not a sixteenth-hearted. And this impressed me. It impressed me *enormously.* That's really all I'm saying here. That I was sorely impressed by it.

Later that evening, after I had left Sandy's cluttered apartment and was back again in my own apartment—I mean in my demented parents' own apartment—safe and sound once again in my salubrious Bastion Of Certitude, I opened up my spiral notebook and then I wrote in it using my best penmanship:

Must bite more nipples. Make circles. Counterclockwise. Right nipple in particular. More responsive than left nipple.
and

The vagina, apparently, is the female sexual organ. However, there is a small hidden nubbin at the end of it which is incredibly sensitive. It is called "the clitoris."

Then I dated the entry and called it a night. It had been quite a night. Very instructive.

***

The following evening I revisited Sandy. Same time. Same place. After I had arrived at Sandy's cluttered apartment—and when I say "cluttered" apartment, what I really mean to say is "book-strewn" or "book-laden" or "book-saturated, bibliophilic" apartment—we immediately sat down on her convertible sofa and proceeded to take up where we had left off. There was no chit-chat this time about the various subtleties of the word Malinla; or about the inherent futility of trying to master the manifold intricacies of Cost Accounting. We were now beyond that—thank goodness. We were now beginning to enter the next phase—what I like to call The Telepathic Phase.

"Hey, Sandy," I said to Sandy then, using my telepathic, psychical abilities in order to communicate to another entity without actually needing to speak to it.

"Yes, Franklin?" she replied in kind.

"I have new math problem for you to solve," I said.

"Oh, goody!" she said. "A new math problem!!"

"Okay. Check this out," I said.

"I can hardly wait," she said.

"If John Q. Public buys a hundred and twenty five shares of Xerox stock at 25 dollar a share...."

"Yes?"

"And if the stock pays a 2% annual dividend quarterly...."

"Yes?"

"And if John's favorite hooker, Portia, charges him 65 dollars an hour for the pleasure of her extremely delightful company...."

"Yes?"

"Then how many hours—rounded to the nearest half hour—could John Q. Public afford to spend with Portia if he sold the stock at 30 dollars a share precisely a year and a half after he'd bought it?"

"So... would that be on June 30th or on July 1st that John Q. Public decides to dump his stock?"

"July 1st."

"Okay. Gotcha."

Sandy considered the problem briefly then—for about five or six pregnant seconds—before expressing to me her reservations concerning the feasibility of her being able to solve it.

"Shit, Franklin," she said to me (wordlessly), "that's a really complicated, nasty math problem!"

"Yeah, Sandy. Tell me about it."

"Why, it's even more complicated and even nastier than the previous 'Alpha Centauri' math problem."

"Yeah, Sandy. Ain't that the truth."

"Well.... This is definitely going to take a while then."

"Yes, Sandy. I expect that it will."

"Well, let's get to it then."

"Yes. Let's."

At that point Sandy closed her eyes and began trying to figure out the new math problem.

***

When I returned home that evening after experimenting sexually with Sandra Scorzo; my alien mind still extremely impressed by Ms. Scorzo's almost Malinlian-like ability to focus; which—if I haven't already mentioned it—is not exactly one of humanity's strong suits; I encountered a kind of difficulty, or a kind of impediment, or a kind of inconvenience, or a kind of frustrating, persnickety obstacle which is generally referred to by most Customer Service Departments throughout the English-speaking civilized world as either "a slight technical problem" or "a glitch." I took the elevator to the sixth floor of my parents' cooperative apartment building of some twelve years, located at 3601 Johnson Avenue in Riverdale, New York—just like I always took it whenever I was returning home from one of my various outings in either The Bronx or Manhattan; got out of the elevator; turned to my right; made a bee line for Apartment 6D; thrust my left hand into my pants pocket; fished around for my apartment keys; took them out and carefully inspected them; and then immediately proceeded to unlock the locks—the first Schlage nickel-plated deadbolt; the second Schlage nickel-plated deadbolt; the third Schlage nickel-plated deadbolt; and then the special floor-mounted "Fox" police lock with its formidable stainless steel pole buttress—guaranteed to stop any miscreant dead in his tracks—from the most floridly psychotic escaped mental patient to the most exquisitely sophisticated professional cat burglar—I unlocked all four of these expensive locks, I say, with the spare keys to my parents' apartment; but was *still*—strangely enough—unable to enter the aforementioned premises. I mean... the door opened up *a little bit*— like... maybe two inches. Two and a half inches.... Three inches....

155

Maybe even four inches. But that was it. Maybe four inches. Four inches! What the fuck, right?

"Hey, Ma!" I called out to my mother at that point through the anywhere-from-two-to-four-inch door opening which the engaged door chain thankfully permitted. "Hey, Einstein! Hey—Genius!" I said. "Take the chain off of the fucking door, will you. How many times do I have to tell you?"

There was nothing, however. No response. Nobody said anything—nobody did anything. Not Ma. Not Dad. Not the neighbors. Oh, forget the neighbors. The neighbors were like... zombies. Zombie neighbors. Zombie debt slaves—just like my father was—the impeccably moral & just zombie debt slave. No. My mother was the real night owl. She'd be up. Not my father.

So I asked her again then. I asked her *nicely*—using my mature, adult, "nice" voice. I said to her:

"Hey, Ma. Do me a favor, would you? Would you take the door chain off of the door, pleeeeze?"

Go away, bum! my mother said to me—finally. *Go back to your whores, bum! Go back to your filthy whorehouses!*

"*What* whorehouses?" I said to my mother.

"You don't think I know?" she said.

"Know what?" I said.

"Don't give me that crap," she said.

"WHAT crap?" I said. "What the hell are you talking about?"

But my mother wouldn't say what. She clammed up again—back to zero again. That's the way it is with these old hags. With these demented ones. With these 'twisted sphinxes.' You meet these 'twisted sphinxes' at the crossroads. And then they tell you shit. Lots of ugly shit. They don't explain themselves. They *never* explain themselves. They just run their 'hag mouths' whenever they feel like it. And then they just leave it to you to clean up the mess.

There was silence at that point. Total silence.

The 'twisted sphinx' was silent—I was also silent.

156

The entire zombie-debt-slave building was silent.

I sighed at that point.

I sighed again—and yet again!—as if the weight of the entire universe had suddenly been dumped upon my puny shoulders.

"Open the door, Ma," I said to my mother again. "Enough with the melodrama. I get it. You're angry."

Go back to your whores, bum! Go back to your disgusting whorehouses! Maybe the whores in your disgusting whorehouses will cook your meals for you and wash your clothes for you!

I sighed again then—for yet a fourth time.

I sure did seem to sigh a lot whenever I was around Ma. That was for damned sure.

Anyway.... Anyway.... Now that it was finally crystal clear to me that what we had on our hands here was not exactly a rational, mentally "together" person; but, rather, an old fashioned 'twisted sphinx' with a mind—and a mouth—made out of chocolate pudding or Silly Putty—what with all of these wild, ridiculous accusations of hers strategically punctuated by belligerent silence—I immediately realized that I had only two options:

Option #1: Do nothing. Do nothing and just stand there. Just stand there like a fucking idiot and be humiliated. Be shit upon.

Option #2: Do something—do *anything*. Doing anything was certainly better than doing nothing, wasn't it? Better to light a single candle than to curse the darkness, says Eleanor Roosevelt. Or was it Confucius who really said that? Or JFK? Or Adlai Stevenson? Or Mother Theresa? Or John Lennon, perhaps? I don't know who actually said it first, but whoever it was definitely has my respect. I mean... it can't be easy being a cockeyed optimist in this floridly psychotic, depraved world of ours. You either have to have experienced far too little—or else far too much—in life in order to stomach mouthing this type of folksy wisdom; and I personally believe—or, rather, I personally would very much *like* to believe—that whoever it was who actually said it first was of the latter, rather than of the former, ilk.

A minute passed....

And then another minute....

And then *another* minute....

And then TEN minutes. Ten fucking minutes wasted exhorting this flying banshee to take the chain off. Madness! Sheer madness! Howling madness! Interminable madness! The interminable madness was just terrible. It was far worse than the interminable bickering—not that the interminable bickering wasn't terrible, mind you—because it was terrible—it was *extremely* terrible—but the interminable madness was even more terrible because the interminable madness was totally gratuitous.

Eleven minutes passed eventually.

Eleven minutes....

Twelve minutes....

Thirteen minutes....

Fourteen minutes....

Fourteen minutes was about enough, I said. Fuck this, I said. Screw you, I said. Screw you and your fucking neurosis, I said—or whatever the hell it is that you call this poison of yours.

Then—just like you'd tell a baby—just like you'd tell a three-year-old baby who was having a really big, humongous temper tantrum in front of the whole goddamned neighborhood—I told the fifty-three-year-old big baby that I was going to give her just ten seconds to stop acting like a complete asshole and to take the fucking chain off of the fucking door. I said to her: "Listen up now, Mrs. Stalin—" (Yes, I actually started calling her "Mrs. Stalin" at this point—"Mrs. Stalin," "Mrs. Hitler," "Mrs. Mussolini," "Mrs. Mao," "Mrs. Pol Pot," "Mrs. Ceausescu," "Mrs. Idi Amin," "Mrs. Caligula.") "—This is your last chance, Mrs. Stalin," I said. "I'm warning you. I'm not kidding around now. Take the chain off of the fucking door, or else I'm going to break the door down. You got that, Josephine?"

I waited. I listened—I listened *carefully*—but there was no answer.

Silence was the only answer. Malicious silence. Vindictive silence. Stony silence that was so thick so that it would have taken a sledgehammer to break through it. And so, in light of this stony silence of hers—this brazenly wanton, totally gratuitous, floridly psychotic, insufferable viciousness—I made good on my final warning to the dyed-in-the-wool, inveterate control freak and natural-born snobby serial soul killer by initiating the countdown sequence:

ONE MISSISSIPPI....

TWO MISSISSIPPI....

THREE MISSISSIPPI....

FOUR MISSISSIPPI....

Still not a peep out of her. More darkness. More blankness. More bleakness. More wretchedness. More anger. More belligerence. More hostility.

More poison.

Where on earth was all of this poison coming from, I wondered? From my mother's *own* mother? From my mother's *own* father? From my maternal grandparents' parents? From *their* grandparents? Their *great*-grandparents? Just how far back exactly in the Cohen family tree did I have to go to find the source of the poison? Shit. Maybe I'd have to go all of the way back to Aaron himself! Maybe *he* was the source of the poison. Maybe *he* was the original poisoner. Maybe the poison was actually biblical in its derivation.

Feeling mostly appalled—and yet at the same time curiously *flattered*, too, at the prospect that something so ugly could have been faithfully passed down through the millennia—I continued now with the countdown:

FIVE MISSISSIPPI....

SIX MISSISSIPPI....

SEVEN MISSISSIPPI....

EIGHT MISSISSIPPI....

When I got to TEN MISSISSIPPI I made good on my promise. I began pounding on the door ferociously. I mean... really *pounding* on it.

Like I was the police or something. You know.... N.Y.P.D., BITCH!
OPEN UP! WE HAVE A SEARCH WARRANT! That kind of
ferocious pounding. If that didn't make it perfectly clear to Ma that I
wasn't fucking around anymore, then I didn't know what would. Sadly,
however—so sadly—so very very very sadly— my mother still refused to
open the door. I mean... she had obviously heard me. How could she
not have heard me? The whole floor had heard me. The whole fucking
building had heard me. Nevertheless.... *Nevertheless*.... There I was, still
in limbo. And there *she* was—still in "Paradise"—that is to say, still in
her nice, comfy, cozy apartment surrounded by all of her nice, comfy,
cozy things... like, for instance, her nice, comfy, cozy poster of
Modigliani's *Gypsy Woman Holding A Baby*; and her nice, comfy, cozy
piano; and her nice, comfy, cozy liquor cabinet; and her nice, comfy,
cozy bookcase filled with all of her nice, comfy, cozy books.... Damn
Ma! Damn that woman! That diseased woman! That demented woman!
You want to know what the *real* gift is that, once you've got it, just
keeps on giving? Here's a hint: It ain't syphilis and it ain't gonorrhea. As
a matter of fact, it's nothing even remotely physical. It's something else.
Something entirely different. And you're looking at it.

You're looking straight at it.

At that point in "the little glitch" or in "the slight technical
difficulty," I had a kind of a *revelation*. Well... not really a revelation. It
was more like a memory. An extra-terrestrial, Malinlian memory of my
early childhood on Planet Earth. Yes. Believe it or not, we do have
them—we extra-terrestrial Malinlian star travelers. I mean memories—I
mean *childhood* memories—just like you un-evolved, reptilian humans
do. We play childrens' games and we read childrens' books; we eat
childrens' food and we wear childrens' clothing. Why, we even have
childrens' schools—although our schools and our teachers do not lie to
our children the way that yours do. We tell them the truth about life's
hardships. About its physical and its emotional challenges.... Its double
standards.... Its shameless hypocrisy.... Indeed, we tell them of things

far worse and far uglier than mere double standards and mere shameless hypocrisy. We do it gently, of course. I mean... we don't try to *scare* them half to death or anything so that they aren't able to have normal, happy, healthy childhoods. We ease them into it. But we still do it.

Anyway.... I had a memory. I had a memory of my childhood dating back to The Sixties. To the early Sixties. 1961, maybe. Suddenly—I don't know why exactly—I was transported back in time through the mysterious vehicle of Memory to that first "claustrophobic," "pinched" Bronx apartment which my earthly mother had found so highly objectionable. On that particular perfectly ordinary, average day— a day pretty much just like any other day in the life of an approximately nine-year-old alien who didn't know yet that he was an alien—I had ensconced myself within my parents' bedroom, where our revered television set was located, thoroughly engrossed in a type of Italian adventure movie—commonly referred to as a "Sword-And-Sandal" or a "Peplum" movie—which portrays the various exploits and tribulations of extremely well known Greco-Roman characters. Like Hercules, for example. Like Perseus, for example. Like Spartacus, for example. Or like Jason and The Argonauts, for example. Biblical stories were told as well in these movies. You know.... The story of David and Goliath.... Samson and Delilah.... Sodom and Gomorrah.... The Queen of Sheba.... This particular "Sword-And-Sandal" movie which the then approximately nine-year-old alien just happened to be so thoroughly engrossed in was about that mythological, epic war which the ancient Greeks had waged against the ancient Trojans. Yes. It was *The Iliad* alright—Immortal Homer on a shoestring budget. Badly written. Badly acted. Badly edited. Badly dubbed. Butchered, really— completely butchered—as only the Italians—God bless 'em—know how to butcher The Immortal Classics.

Now, throughout the entirety of this... extravaganza—this exceedingly original cinematic interpretation of one of the cornerstones of Western Literature—whose intended audience, by the way, was basically your typical pre-pubescent Dennis The Menace.... All throughout this exciting film, I say, the Trojans—those dirty bastards—had defended their beleaguered homeland against the vastly superior Grecian forces with extreme cruelty and with extreme treachery, using all sorts of dirty tactics: pouring boiling oil, for instance, over the Grecian soldiers whenever they got too close to the gates of the city; or by making believe that they wanted to end the war by inviting all of the high-ranking Grecian officials to an elaborate dinner at the Trojan palace—only to slaughter them as they sat down to eat. Shit like that. Nasty shit. Vile shit. Trojan shit. Only... Hector was gone now—the "favorite son" of The Trojan People; having been shockingly, ignominiously vanquished in a veritable show-stopping "duel to the death" by the half-man / half-god indomitable offspring of Peleus and Thetis. The death of Hector heralded the end for Troy—for without its charismatic, imperturbable leader to rally its forces and to boost its morale, all hope was now abandoned for a glorious—if not a speedy—victory. Already the jubilant, pertinacious Greeks were beginning to self-assemble in horrific numbers—like a swarm of agitated, incensed bees—by the Trojan ramparts and fortifications; and once the jubilant, pertinacious Greeks had finally succeeded in breaching those ramparts and fortifications, well... then that would be it for those dirty rotten sneaky bastards. The City of Troy would fall hard then—very hard—instantaneously, even. Fires would be lit; women would be raped; men would be slaughtered; and riches would be plundered—which was all pretty much standard operating procedure in any civilized, respectable "sacking process."

Now there was one particular scene in the movie. I guess you could call it the movie's climax or *denouement*. In that scene, one of the Grecian generals—I think it was Odysseus if I'm not mistaken—said to all of the other generals while they were all milling around inside of a huge tent which, I suppose, served the Grecians as a kind of "make-shift" War Room.... Suddenly—as I say—Odysseus said to all of the other generals something like... "Hey, guys! I just had a brainstorm!"

"Oh, yeah?" they said to him.

"Yeah. That's right," he said to them.

"So? You gonna share it with us or do we have to guess, Odysseus?"

"No. I'll share it with you."

"Well, go ahead then."

At that point all of the other Grecian generals shut their pie holes and just listened intently.

Odysseus said to them then:

"What do you say we build us a battering ram, fellas?"

"A battering ram?"

"Yeah. A battering ram. You know…. To break through the Trojan gates 'n shit."

"You mean… you don't want us to build a horse, Odysseus?"

"A *horse?*"

"Yeah."

"Well, what for?"

"You know…. To give to the enemy. As a kind of a peace offering."

"Peace offering?"

"Yeah. Don't you remember, Odysseus? We build 'em this big wooden horse—see?—which is hollow inside. Hollow enough to stow away twenty or thirty of our best guys, anyway. Then, after we build it, we leave the horse at the Trojan gates. They say: 'Oh, look! A horsee! What a pretty gift from those clever Grecians!' Then they open the gates up, they drag the horsee inside, and then—voila!—we kill 'em."

"I don't like it," said Odysseus. "It's too complicated."

"Too complicated?"

"Yeah. It's too complicated. Too… arty fartsy. It'll never work."

"But you said it *would* work!"

"Did I? *Really?*"

"Yeah. You said it was like… the best brainstorm you ever had."

"Hey, what can I tell you, fellas? Sometimes I'm hot and sometimes I'm not. I guess that time I wasn't."

"What?"

"Hot."

"Oh."

"Mea culpa."

"So... no horse, then?"

"No, no horsee. Think battering ram. Think a big, motherfucking battering ram. That'll teach those Trojan bastards a lesson."

And so that's exactly what the Greeks did in the movie. They decided to scrap The Trojan Horse Concept in favor of The Big, Motherfucking Battering Ram Concept. And—needless to say—they built their big, motherfucking battering ram using only the finest, sturdiest timbers available: alder, spruce, conifer, pine, walnut, beech, hickory—you name it. Hell. They even chopped down some of their tallest ship masts and bound them together with what looked like laundry rope. That sounded pretty good to me. That sounded really classical. I mean... if The Greeks had been able to do it approximately Twelve Hundred B.C., I said to myself as I stood in the hallway, then why can't *I* do it approximately Two Thousand A.D.? The Greeks had *their* obstacles? Well... I've got *my* obstacles. The Greeks had *their* enemies? Well... I've got mine, too! And so with a cool, measured, even stride, I stepped back a few paces from the extremely flimsy & inexpensive and yet at the same time curiously durable, resilient door chain—just as the Greeks had stepped back from the Trojan barriers which protected Ilium. And when my distance from the reviled door chain was deemed to be sufficiently adequate so as to enable my battering-ram-like Grecian body to achieve the requisite levels of Homeric momentum, I ran back to the reviled door chain with all of the swiftness of an Olympian sprinter; and with all of the fierceness of a Spartan hoplite; and with all of the guile of a Circean sorceress; and with all of the superhuman, incredible endurance of The Great Demi-God, Sir Ernest Shackleton; pretending that I, too, was an ancient battering ram constructed from ancient timbers and from ancient ship masts.

6. OUT OF THE FRYING PAN AND INTO THE FIRE

After I had finally succeeded in ripping the fucking door chain off of the fucking door of The Two Nut Jobs' fucking apartment, and then entering the premises in fucking triumph, things started getting... interesting.

First off of the bat, my parents got a registered letter from the Board of Directors of *The New Windsor Cooperative Apartment Building*, informing them that the demolition—or that even the *proposed* demolition—of New Windsor Cooperative property without the express consent of the cooperative shareholders was in violation of Article 18, Section 3b of *The New Windsor Cooperative Bylaws*; and that— furthermore—as clearly indicated in Article 18, Section 3c of said bylaws, such unacceptable and deviant behavior was punishable by A) trans-orbital lobotomy and/or B) testicular electrocution and/or C) public stoning and/or D) cattle prod up the ass. My father waved the letter in front of my face. It was serious. Pretty serious. At the end of the letter there were multiple signatures—angry signatures—irate signatures— followed at the bottom of the last page by the words SENT CERTIFIED— RETURN RECEIPT REQUESTED IMMEDIATELY!

"Well? What have you got to say for yourself?" my father said to me after he had read me the letter. "It says here on Page 3 that they're going to charge me eleven hundred seventy dollars for this infantile little stunt of yours. Eleven hundred seventy dollars, Franklin.... ELEVEN HUNDRED SEVENTY DOLLARS!"

"Gee, Dad. That's seems like an awful lot of money to me."

"Yeah, tell me about it, fuck face. It's not 'an awful lot.' It's *an obscene lot!*"

"I mean... it's *only* a busted door, Dad. It's not like they're going to be performing brain surgery or anything...."

"WHAT THE HELL DO YOU KNOW ABOUT BRAIN SURGERY? WHAT THE HELL DO YOU KNOW ABOUT *ANYTHING?*"

"Well, at least I know enough to take the door chain off of the fucking door when my fucking children fucking ask me to do it. How about *that*, Genius? Does that qualify as 'knowing anything?'" Okay, okay. I didn't actually say that. I kept my trap shut. But I was certainly thinking it. I was thinking: "Who cares if you're pissed, Dad? So be pissed. Be very pissed! But being pissed still isn't going to change the fact that I'm a Grecian winner and that you're a Trojan loser. It's that simple. So get over it, asshole."

I didn't say that to my father either, however.

So much for The Paternal Nut Job....

The Maternal Nut Job, on the other hand—unlike her exceedingly articulate masculine counterpart—started immediately making like Helen Keller. Not a peep out of her. Not a word. Not a syllable. Not even a *half* syllable. For a couple of seconds there, I thought I was hallucinating or something. Was having a nervous breakdown or something. Died, maybe, and had gone to heaven or something. She was that quiet. Hallelujah!

That evening I wrote in my journal: "General contractor coming Tuesday AM. Locksmith coming Tuesday PM. Building inspector reassessing Thursday. Dad pissed. Ma mute. Silence golden. Silence glorious. Don't know how long, however, glorious silence is going to last. Best estimate: two days. Three, maybe. Four—tops. Using lull to read N. now. *BGAE*. Part Nine. Section 289. Say what you like about N., the way he uses language is just extraordinary. M. is a joke compared to this guy. A clumsy elephant. An earnest plodder. Always goes from Point A to Point B in a straight line. Never deviates. God forbid that he should ever deviate! That he should ever dance a little. That he should ever *sing* a little. Have some fun with words every once in a while instead of treating words as if they were just disposable toilet paper. These M. characters all make me sick—what with their insipid promises of an essentially Christian afterlife—only not in the next world, but right here in *this* one. It's the same old story, told by the same old control freaks: Paradise NOW! Utopia NOW! Conformity NOW! Obedience NOW!

'The road to hell,' so the saying goes, 'is paved with good intentions.' Only where exactly are the good intentions here? I see the 'hell' part alright—only not so much the 'good intentions' part."

At that point I started thinking seriously about getting the hell out of the insane asylum. Out of Bellevue, I mean. Out of Bedlam, I mean. Out of The Sunnybrook State Mental Hospital For The Criminally Harvard-Fixated And Terminally Word-Obsessed. That was the general plan, anyway. To escape all of the gratuitous madness—for it was all gratuitous—all completely unnecessary. And so to that end, I began strategizing—planning my "Great Escape" from within The Bastion Of Certitude. Also, over the weekends, I would take little forays into The Big Apple. Little outings. Little excursions. These little excursions of mine into The Big Apple were tremendously important to me. Yes.... *Exceptionally* important to me—for my entire strategy was dependent upon them. It was one thing, after all, to *theoretically* plan "The Great Escape" from within the relative safety of The Bastion Of Certitude; quite another, however, to abandon The Bastion, and to do some actual "hands on" reconnoitering.—And so that's exactly what I would do on these nifty little weekend excursions of mine. I would "reconnoiter." I would "scout the territory." I would get on the #1 Train at Broadway & 231st Street—which was by far the cheapest way for me to get to Manhattan—whereupon, after thirty minutes or so of having the first three of my five senses continually pummeled and continually violated— of having my sense of sight continually pummeled and violated; of having my sense of hearing continually pummeled and violated; of having my sense of smell (particularly this last one) continually pummeled and continually violated by unabashed, brazen squalor—I would exit the train at 96th Street. From there, I would walk. I would just… walk. Like some yokel; like some hayseed. Like some farm boy from The Midwest visiting The Big Apple for the first time. I would walk Uptown and I would walk Downtown. I would walk East and I would walk West. It didn't really matter where I chose to walk on these little fact-finding, secret "missions" of mine just as long as I was walking *somewhere*. Away from the madness. Away from the nut house.

***

One day, on the fourth weekend of my various comings and goings about The Isle Of Manhattan, I found myself walking along a great boulevard called "Columbus Avenue." It was around 10 o'clock of a Saturday morning in late March or in early April. The sky was blue. It was a brilliant blue—cerulean blue, if I'm not mistaken. And since I myself was kind of a brilliant guy whose favorite colors in the entire universe were A) cerulean blue and B) ultramarine blue, I took note of the sky; I took particular note of it. And then, having finished noting it—and having finished noting it, as I have just indicated, *exceedingly well*—with *meticulous* precision—devoting considerably more than just the usual millisecond to its contemplation and to its admiration—I was just about to scoot down to yet *another* boulevard known as "Amsterdam Avenue" in order to buy myself a bottle of Coca-Cola and a bag of Utz Kettle Classic Potato Chips—my usual brunch during these weekend excursions—when all of a sudden, out of nowhere—I mean literally *nowhere*—IT materialized. Yes…. It was an anachronism alright. From a different age—from The Age Of Dinosaurs. It stood out from the other apartment buildings to the right of it and to the left of it like a brontosaurus in a petting zoo. Or like a leper in a Miss America contest. It was that strange. And it was that fascinating. I approached the leper— I mean, the dinosaur. I walked up the front steps and I opened the glass door. Then I approached an old man with a long beard. I presumed that the old man with the long beard was either the building's owner or else the building's landlord. I presumed correctly. He was the building's owner. Then I asked the old man with the long beard if he had a room to let, to which he replied:

"What kind of a room, sonny boy?"

"Oh.... Any room."

"*Any* room?"

"Yeah. Any room will do just fine."

The old man looked at me oddly then. He kind of... pricked up his ears then and studied me carefully, as if he had just stumbled across a chest of gold doubloons and wanted to make sure that he wasn't dreaming.

"What are you staring at?" I said to the old man.

"Who's staring?" he said.

"You are," I said.

"Sorry," he said. "No offense. It's just that we don't get too many... philosophers here."

"How do you know that I'm a philosopher?"

"Oh, I don't know," he said. "Just a hunch, I guess...."

I didn't like this old man. I didn't like anything about the guy. He reminded me of my Uncle Seymour, who was always urging me to go to Law School. And he smelled, too—just like Uncle Sy smelled. It was a fetid smell. An unhygienic smell—like that of a sickly man who didn't bathe enough; or who was incontinent; or who wore an ostomy appliance. But then again, Uncle Sy was a widower. Hadn't married again after the wife passed. So maybe that was it. No female to pester him. To wash his clothes for him, and tell him his hygiene sucked....

The old man showed me a room then on the sixth floor—which was the top floor. And what a room it was! What a beautiful room! It had a bed. It had a blanket. It had a chair. It had a desk. It had a mirror. It had a closet. It had a chest of drawers. Why... it had EVERYTHING! Everything you could possibly ask for. No frilly stuff. Just the basics. Oh, I loved that room! I loved it dearly! I pictured myself doing terrific things in it. Writing terrific poems. Writing terrific stories. Writing terrific novels. Shaking the world up.... And then I had to pause, unfortunately—albeit momentarily—in these rainbow-colored, misty dreams of mine as reality suddenly smashed into me like the glistening grill of a Mack truck.

"Does it have a toilet, Mister?" I said to the old man.

"What?"

"I said does it have a toilet? Does it have a bathroom?"

"Of course it does. It has *six* bathrooms."

"Six, huh?"

"One on every floor."

"Well, where's the one on this floor?"

"End of the hall, sonny. On your left."

I started walking down the long hallway.

Half way down it, I ran into Ted.

"Well, hi there!" Ted said to me. "My name is Ted. What's your name?"

"Franklin," I said to Ted.

"Well, it's a real pleasure to meet you, Franklin."

"Yeah. Likewise." I said to Ted.

"Say, Franklin...." Ted said to me then.

"Yes, Ted?" I said to Ted.

"You wouldn't happen to have twenty dollars on you, would you, Franklin?"

"No, I'm afraid not, Ted," I said to Ted.

"Gee, that's too bad," Ted said to me then. "Well, how about ten dollars? Have you got ten dollars?"

"Sorry, Ted. I don't have ten dollars either."

"Well, how about five then? Surely you must have *five* dollars?"

"Sorry, Ted, but I don't have any money."

"Gee. That's a shame, Franklin."

"Yeah. Isn't it, Ted? Don't you just hate it when you don't have any money?"

Ted smiled at me then—and I smiled back at Ted.

He seemed like a nice enough sort of fellow. A little pushy perhaps—but nice, basically.

I don't know why exactly, but something told me that I was going to be seeing a lot more of this "Ted" person.

When I returned from the bathroom, the room was still there—thank God!—just as beautiful and just as amazing and just as piss-poor as when I'd first laid eyes on it. Same bed. Same blanket. Same chair. Same desk. Same mirror. Same closet. Same chest of drawers. Same everything! Already I was thinking of writing a novel about it. Hadn't even rented the room yet, but already—a novel. The novel would be called "The Beautiful Room" and it would be a beautiful tale about a beautiful space traveler who had been marooned, unfortunately—through no fault of his own, mind you—on an exceedingly unevolved, savage planet with little to no hope at all of becoming anything else but what it already was. The planet which he had been marooned on was called THE EARTH; and he had been instantaneously transported there—down to this exceedingly unevolved, savage planet—from another, far more advanced, planet; situated in the general vicinity of the constellation known as Orion. Oh, what a beautiful planet his own planet had been! Its inhabitants were extremely beautiful—both spiritually as well as physically speaking; and the things they did there, extremely beautiful; and the thoughts they thought there, extremely beautiful; and their capacity to discern The Beautiful even in the midst of extreme ugliness.... Beautiful.... Just beautiful.... Only now, unfortunately, he was marooned here—on this unevolved, savage planet inhabited by mostly unevolved, savage creatures—and there wasn't a damned thing which he could do about it. The only thing which he could really do about it was to try to accept his fate with equanimity. With "class," as they say. With "grace." Which meant trying not to be angry about it. Which meant trying not to be bitter about it. Which—believe me—wasn't easy since there was so much to be angry and bitter about. That would be the plot of the novel: trying to avoid anger, to

171

avoid bitterness. Trying to turn base lead—just like the ancient alchemists—into a solid gold brick shit house. Now... mind you: I didn't know exactly how I was going to begin this... misanthropic novel of mine; because the beginnings of most serious novels—whether they be misanthropic or philanthropic—are usually exceedingly difficult, if not downright impossible. There are always so many false starts and blind alleys; so many failed attempts and dead ends. So—no. I didn't know exactly how I was actually going to start the novel—what specific path I was actually going to take in order to get me headed in the right direction. I mean, you can only determine that through trial and error; by writing tons of stuff and then by discarding most of it. But I sure as hell knew how I was going to *end* the novel. I was going to end it brutally—with brutal honesty—without sugar-coating it, as do so many others.

I was going to end it by writing:

No, The Earth is not worst of all possible worlds. But, then again, it sure as hell isn't the best of 'em either. Nobody asks you whether you want to be born on it, just as nobody asks you whether you want to die on it either. You just wake up one morning and you say to yourself: "Well... I'm here now. So this is it, huh? So this is what I have to work with, huh? Hm...." And then—once you've said it—you pretty much know everything— everything, that is, that you can know. The rest, my friends, is just noise. Noise and more noise. God! There's so much noise here. Just try to tune the noise out as best as you can. Whenever you can. And don't forget to listen to Beethoven.

Photo: Irene Levanos

About the author:

Richard Leiter lives in a house—somewhere. Richard Leiter sits at the computer in his house every day, where he tries to write as well as he can. Most of what he writes is garbage. The extremely small amount which he thinks may *not* be garbage he puts away inside of a hanging folder. Then he waits. He just...waits. He lets time pass. Sometimes lots of time. Then, when he takes the hanging folder out again and re-reads what he has placed inside of it, he realizes that most of that was garbage, too. Not all of it, mind you. But *almost* all of it. Richard Leiter thinks that this is no way to live. Richard Leiter thinks that Plato got it all wrong. Richard Leiter thinks that The Examined Life is not all that it's cracked up to be.

When Richard Leiter is not sitting at the computer in his house trying to write as well as he can, he does the same things which most people do. He has to work for a living; pays bills; gets the usual unending stream of junk mail and irritating phone calls from telemarketers asking him for money; and he worries a lot about the direction his life is going in.

Amazingly, it only took Mr. Leiter a mere twenty years to write *Leaving Home.* He is currently working on a sequel to it. This one should go even faster.

www.ingramcontent.com/pod-product-compliance
Lightning Source LLC
Chambersburg PA
CBHW030336030726
47499CB00003B/796